CRY, THE
COUN

A Story of Comf

by
ALAN PATON

Abridged and very lightly simplified by
G. F. WEAR and R. H. DURHAM

Hope Byram
Lobatse
1980

LONGMAN

LONGMAN GROUP UK LIMITED
Longman House, Burnt Mill,
Harlow, Essex CM20 2JE, England
and Associated Companies throughout the world

School Edition

First published 1953
This impression 1988

The publishers are indebted to Messrs Jonathan Cape Ltd
and Mr Alan Paton for permission to use this edition

Produced by Longman Group (FE) Ltd
Printed in Hong Kong

ISBN 0-582-53009-1

THE BRIDGE SERIES

The *Bridge Series* offers interesting reading matter for the students of English as a second or foreign language who have reached a stage between the graded supplementary reader and full English. Having enjoyed a number of books in the *Simplified English Series* such a student is ready for something more challenging.

The books in the *Bridge Series* are moderately simplified in vocabulary and often slightly reduced in length. Nearly all retain the syntax of the original writers. This has the dual advantage of giving practice in understanding more advanced sentence patterns and making it possible to keep the original flavour of the book.

Of intermediate difficulty between the *Simplified English Series* and the unrestricted English of literature, the *Bridge Series* books contain little of vocabulary or idiom that is not immediately valuable to the fairly advanced learner, and we hope that they will prove thoroughly enjoyable to read and study for their own sakes.

Technical Note

The vocabulary of the *Simplified English Series* is the 2,000 words of the *General Service list (Interim Report on Vocabulary Selection)* and there is a degree of structure control. In the *Bridge Series* words outside the commonest 7,000 (in Thorndike and Lorge: *A Teacher's Handbook of 30,000 Words,* Columbia University, 1944) have usually been replaced by commoner and more generally useful words. Words used which are outside the first 3,000 of the list are explained in a glossary and are so distributed throughout the book that they do not occur at a greater density than 25 per running 1,000 words.

AUTHOR'S NOTE

No person in this book is intended to be an actual person. Nor in any event of the story is reference intended to any actual event: except that the accounts of the boycott of the buses, the building of Shanty Town, the finding of gold at Odendaalsrust, and the miners' strike, are a mixture of truth and fiction. In these ways therefore the story is not true, but considered as a social record it is the plain and simple truth.

The population of South Africa is about eleven millions. Of these about two and a half million are white, of whom roughly three-fifths are Afrikaans-speaking and two-fifths English-speaking. The rest, except for one million coloured people, by which we mean of mixed white and other blood, are the black people of the African tribes.

BOOK ONE

1

THERE is a lovely road that runs from Ixopo into the hills. These hills are grass-covered and rolling, and they are lovely beyond any singing of it. The road climbs seven miles into them, to Carisbrooke; and from there, if there is no mist, you look down on one of the fairest valleys of Africa. About you there is grass and you may hear the forlorn crying of the titihoya, one of the birds of the veld. Below you is the valley of the Umzimkulu, on its journey from the Drakensberg Mountains to the sea; and, beyond and behind the river, great hill after great hill; and beyond and behind them, the mountains of Ingeli and East Griqualand.

The grass is rich and thick; you cannot see the soil. It holds the rain and the mist, and they sink slowly into the ground, feeding the streams in every small valley. It is well looked after, and not too many cattle feed upon it; not too many fires burn it, laying bare the soil. Stand barefoot upon it, for the ground is holy, being even as it came from God. Keep it, guard it, care for it, for it keeps men, guards men, cares for men. Destroy it and man is destroyed.

Where you stand the grass is rich and thick; you cannot see the soil. But the rich green hills break down. They fall to the valley below, and, falling, change their nature. For they grow red and bare; they cannot hold the rain and mist, and the streams are dry in the small valleys. Too many

3

cattle feed upon the grass, and too many fires have burned it. Do not stand barefoot upon it, for it is coarse and sharp, and the stones cut under the feet. It is not kept, or guarded, or cared for; it no longer keeps men, guards men, cares for men. The titihoya does not cry here any more.

The great red hills stand desolate, and the earth has torn away like flesh. The lightning flashes over them, the clouds pour down upon them, the dead streams come to life, full of the red blood of the earth. Down in the valleys women scratch the soil that is left, and the maize hardly reaches the height of a man. They are valleys of old men and old women, of mothers and children. The men are away, the young men and the girls are away. The soil cannot keep them any more.

2

The small child ran importantly to the wood-and-iron church with the letter in her hand. Next to the church was a house and she knocked timidly on the door. The Reverend Stephen Kumalo looked up from the table where he was writing, and he called, "Come in."

The small child opened the door, carefully, like one who is afraid to open carelessly the door of so important a house, and stepped timidly in.

"I bring a letter, umfundisi."

"A letter, eh? Where did you get it, my child?"

"From the store, umfundisi. The white man asked me to bring it to you."

"That was good of you. Go well, small one."

But she did not go at once. She rubbed one bare foot against the other, she rubbed one finger along the edge of the umfundisi's table.

"Perhaps you might be hungry, small one."

"Not very hungry, umfundisi."

"Perhaps a little hungry."

"Yes, a little hungry, umfundisi."

"Go to the mother then. Perhaps she has some food."

"I thank you, umfundisi."

She walked delicately, as though her feet might do harm in so great a house, a house with tables and chairs, and a clock, and a plant in a pot, and many books, more even than the books at the school.

Kumalo looked at his letter. It was dirty. It had been in many hands, no doubt. It came from Johannesburg; now there in Johannesburg were many of his own people. His brother John, who was a carpenter, had gone there, and had a business of his own in Sophiatown, Johannesburg. His sister Gertrude, twenty-five years younger than he, and the child of his parents' old age, had gone there with her small son to look for the husband who had never come back from the mines. His only child Absalom had gone there, to look for his aunt Gertrude, and he had never returned. And indeed many other relatives were there, though none so near as these. It was hard to say from whom this letter came, for it was so long since any of these had written that one did not well remember their writing.

He turned the letter over, but there was nothing to show from whom it came. He was unwilling to open it, for, once such a thing is opened, it cannot be shut again.

He called to his wife, "Has the child gone?"

"She is eating, Stephen."

"Let her eat then. She brought a letter. Do you know anything about a letter?"

"How should I know, Stephen?"

"No, that I do not know. Look at it."

She took the letter and she felt it. But there was nothing

in the touch of it to tell from whom it might be. She read
out the address slowly and carefully:

> *Rev. Stephen Kumalo,*
>   *St. Mark's Church,*
>   *Ndotsheni,*
>   *NATAL.*

She gathered up her courage, and said, "It is not from
our son."

"No," he said. And he sighed. "It is not from our
son."

"Perhaps it concerns him," she said.

"Yes," he said. "That may be so."

"It is not from Gertrude," she said.

"Perhaps it is my brother John."

"It is not from John," she said.

They were silent, and she said, "How we desire such a
letter, and when it comes, we fear to open it."

"Who is afraid?" he said. "Open it."

She opened it, slowly and carefully, for she did not open
many letters. She spread it out open, and read it slowly
and carefully, so that he did not hear all that she said.

"Read it aloud," he said.

She read it aloud, reading as a Zulu who reads English.

> "THE MISSION HOUSE,
>   SOPHIATOWN,
>   JOHANNESBURG.
>   *September 25th,* 1946.

MY DEAR BROTHER IN CHRIST,

      I have had the experience of
meeting a young woman here in Johannesburg. Her
name is Gertrude Kumalo, and I understand she is the

sister of the Rev. Stephen Kumalo, St. Mark's Church, Ndotsheni. This young woman is very sick, and therefore I ask you to come quickly to Johannesburg. Come to the Rev. Theophilus Msimangu, the Mission House, Sophiatown, and there I shall give you some advice. I shall also find a place for you to live, where the expenditure will not be very serious.

I am, dear brother in Christ,

Yours faithfully,

THEOPHILUS MSIMANGU."

They were both silent till at long last she spoke.

" Well, my husband? "

" Yes, what is it? "

" This letter, Stephen. You have heard it now."

" Yes, I have heard it. It is not an easy letter."

" It is not an easy letter. What will you do? "

" Has the child eaten? "

She went to the kitchen and came back with the child.

" Have you eaten, my child? "

" Yes, umfundisi."

" Then go well, my child. And thank you for bringing the letter."

" Stay well, umfundisi. Stay well, mother."

" Go well, my child."

So the child went delicately to the door, and shut it behind her gently, letting the handle turn slowly like one who fears to let it turn fast.

When the child had gone, she said to him, " What will you do, Stephen? "

" About what, my wife? "

She said patiently to him, " About this letter, Stephen."

He sighed. " Bring me the St. Chad's money," he said.

She went out, and came back with a tin, of the kind in

which they sell coffee, and this she gave to him. He held it in his hand, studying it, as though there might be some answer in it, till at last she said, " It must be done, Stephen."

" How can I use it? " he said. " This money was to send Absalom to St. Chad's College."

" Absalom will never go now to St. Chad's."

" How can you say that? " he said sharply. " How can you say such a thing? "

" He is in Johannesburg," she said wearily. " When people go to Johannesburg, they do not come back."

" You have said it," he said. " It is said now. This money which was saved for that purpose will never be used for it. You have opened a door, and because you have opened it, we must go through. And God alone knows where we shall go."

" It was not I who opened it," she said, hurt by his accusation. " It has a long time been open, but you would not see."

" We had a son," he said harshly. " Zulus have many children, but we had only one son. He went to Johannesburg, and as you said—when people go to Johannesburg, they do not come back. They do not go to St. Chad's, to learn that knowledge without which no black man can live. They go to Johannesburg, and there they are lost, and no one hears of them at all. And this money . . ."

" You are hurting yourself," she said.

" Hurting myself? Hurting myself? I do not hurt myself, it is they who are hurting me. My own son, my own sister, my own brother. They go away and they do not write any more. Perhaps it does not seem to them that we suffer. Perhaps they do not care for it." His voice rose into loud and angry words, till she cried out at him, " You are hurting me also."

He came to himself and said to her humbly, " That I

may not do." He held out the tin to her. "Open it," he said.

With trembling hands she took the tin and opened it. She emptied it out over the table; some old and dirty notes, and a flood of silver and copper. She counted it slowly.

"Twelve pounds, five shillings and seven pence."

"I shall take," he said, "eight pounds, and the shillings and pence."

"Take it all, Stephen. There may be doctors, hospitals, other troubles. Take it all. And take the Post Office Book —there is ten pounds in it—you must take that also."

"I have been saving that for your stove," he said.

"That cannot be helped," she said. "And that other money, though we saved it for St. Chad's, I had meant it for your new black clothes, and a new black hat, and new white collars."

"That cannot be helped either. Let me see, I shall go . . ."

"To-morrow," she said. "From Carisbrooke."

He rose heavily to his feet, and went and stood before her. "I am sorry I hurt you," he said. "I shall go and pray in the church."

He went out of the door, and she watched him through the little window, walking slowly to the door of the church. Then she sat down at his table, and put her head on it, and was silent, with the patient suffering of black women, with the suffering of oxen, with the suffering of any that are mute.

. . . .

All roads lead to Johannesburg. Through the long nights the trains pass to Johannesburg. The lights of the swaying coach fall on the grass and the stones of a country that sleeps. Happy the eyes that can close.

3

It is interesting to wait for the train at Carisbrooke, while it climbs up out of the great valley. Those who know can tell you with each whistle where it is, at what road, what farm, what river. But though Stephen Kumalo has been there a full hour before he need, he does not listen to these things. This is a long way to go, and a lot of money to pay. And who knows how sick his sister may be, and what money that may cost? And if he has to bring her back, what will that cost too? And Johannesburg is a great city, with so many streets they say that a man can spend his days going up one and down another, and never the same one twice. One must catch buses too, but not as here, where the only bus that comes is the right bus. For there, there is a multitude of buses, and only one bus in ten, one bus in twenty maybe, is the right bus. If you take the wrong bus, you may travel to quite some other place. And they say it is dangerous to cross the street, yet one must needs cross it. For there a woman of Ndotsheni, who had gone there when her husband was dying, saw her son killed in the street. Twelve years old and moved by excitement, he stepped out into danger, but she hesitated and stayed still. And under her eyes the great lorry crushed the life out of her son.

And the great fear too—the greatest fear since it was so seldom spoken. Where was their son? Why did he not write any more?

There is a last whistle and the train is near at last.

As all country trains in South Africa are, it was full of black travellers. On this train indeed there were not many others, for the Europeans of this district all have their cars, and hardly travel by train any more. Kumalo climbed into the carriage for non-Europeans, already full of the humbler people of his race. The day was warm, and the smell strong in the carriage. But Kumalo was a humble man, and did not much care. The train whistled and jerked. Kumalo was nearly thrown off his feet. The journey had begun.

And now the fear back again, the fear of the unknown, the fear of the great city where boys were killed crossing the street, the fear of Gertrude's sickness. Deep down the fear for his son. Deep down the fear of a man who lives in a world not made for him, whose own world is slipping away, dying, being destroyed, beyond any recall.

The humble man reached in his pocket for his sacred book, and began to read. It was this world alone that was certain.

4

The train thundered on all through the night and Kumalo awoke in the swaying coach to the half-light before the dawn.

This is a new country, a strange country, rolling and rolling away as far as the eye can see. There are new names here, hard for a Zulu who has been schooled in English. For they are in the language that is called Afrikaans, a language that he has never yet heard spoken.

"The mines," the men in the carriage cry. "The mines." For many of them are going to work in the mines.

"Are these the mines, those white flat hills in the distance?"

"That is the rock out of the mines, umfundisi. The gold has been taken out of it."

"How does the rock come out?"

"We go down under the ground and dig it out,

umfundisi. And when it is hard to dig, we go away, and the white men blow it out with the fire-sticks. Then we come back and clear it away; we load it, and it goes up in a cage."

"How does it go up?"

"It is wound up by a great wheel. There is a wheel, umfundisi, there is a wheel."

A great iron structure rising into the air, and a great wheel above it. Great buildings, and steam blowing out of pipes, and men hurrying about. An endless procession of trucks, motor cars, lorries, buses, one great confusion.

"Is that Johannesburg?" he asks. They laugh.

"That is nothing," they say. "In Johannesburg there are buildings, so high——" But they cannot describe them.

Railway-lines, railway-lines, it is a wonder. To the left, to the right, so many that he cannot count. A train rushes past them, with a sudden roaring of sound that makes him jump in his seat. The buildings get higher, the streets more uncountable. How does one find one's way in such a confusion? It is dusk, and the lights are coming on in the streets. One of the men points for him. "Johannesburg, umfundisi."

He sees great high buildings. The train stops, under a great roof, and there are thousands of people. Steps go down into the earth, and here is a tunnel under the ground. Black people, white people, some going, some coming, so many that the tunnel is full. He comes out into a great hall, and goes up the steps, and here he is out in the street. The noise is immense. Cars and buses one behind the other, more than he has ever imagined. His heart beats like that of a child.

"God watch over me," he says to himself. "God watch over me."

.   .   .   .

A young man came to him and said, "Where do you want to go, umfundisi?"

"To Sophiatown, young man."

"Come with me then and I shall show you."

He was grateful for this kindness, but half of him was afraid. He was confused by the many turnings that they made under the high buildings, but at last they came to a place of many buses.

"You must stand in the line, umfundisi. Have you your money for the ticket?"

Quickly, eagerly, as though he must show this young man that he appreciated his kindness, he put down his bag and took out his purse. He was nervous to ask how much it was, and took a pound from the purse.

"Shall I get the ticket for you, umfundisi? Then you need not lose your place in the line, while I go to the ticket office."

"Thank you," he said.

The young man took the pound and walked a short distance to the corner. As he turned it, Kumalo was afraid. The line moved forward and he with it, clutching his bag. And again forward, and again forward, and soon he must enter a bus, but still he had no ticket. He left the line, and walked to the corner, but there was no sign of the young man. He sought courage to speak to someone, and went to an elderly man, decently and cleanly dressed.

"Where is the ticket office, my friend?"

"What ticket office, umfundisi?"

"For the ticket for the bus."

"You get your ticket on the bus. There is no ticket office."

The man looked a decent man, and the priest spoke to him humbly. "I gave a pound to a young man," he said, "and he told me he would get my ticket at the ticket office."

"You have been cheated, umfundisi. Can you see the young man? No, you will not see him again. Look, come with me. Where are you going, Sophiatown?"

"Yes, Sophiatown. To the Mission House."

"Oh yes. I know it well. I shall come with you myself. Do you know the Reverend Msimangu?"

"Indeed, I have a letter from him."

They again took the last place in the line, and in time they took their places in the bus. They got off at a small street and walked a great distance until at last they stopped before a lighted house, and knocked. The door was opened by a tall young man in priest's dress.

"Mr. Msimangu, I bring a friend to you, the Reverend Kumalo from Ndotsheni."

"Come in, come in, my friends. Mr. Kumalo, I am glad to greet you. You are no doubt hungry, Mr. Kumalo. Mr. Mafolo, will you stay for some food?"

But Mr. Mafolo would not wait. The door shut after him, and Kumalo settled himself in a big chair. The room was light, the great bewildering town was shut out, and Kumalo was thankful. The long journey to Johannesburg was over, and he had taken a liking to this young, confident man. In good time no doubt they would come to discuss the reason for his journey. For the moment it was enough to feel welcome and secure.

5

"I have a place for you to sleep, my friend, in the house of an old woman, a Mrs. Lithebe, who is a good member of our church. It is cheap there, and you can have your meals with us here, in the Mission."

They went into a room where a table was laid and there

he met many priests, both black and white, and they sat down after a prayer and ate together. He sat next to a young rosy-cheeked priest from England, who asked him where he came from, and what it was like there. And another black priest cried out, "I am also from Ixopo. My father and mother are still alive there. How is it there?"

And he told them all about these places, of the great hills and valleys of that far country. And the love of them must have been in his voice, for they were all silent and listened to him. He told them too of the sickness of the land, and how the grass had disappeared; how it was a land of old men and women, and mothers and children; how the maize grew barely to the height of a man; how the tribe was broken, and the house broken, and the man broken; how, when they went away, many never came back, many never wrote any more. How this was true not only in Ndotsheni, but also in many other districts. But of Gertrude and Absalom he said nothing.

So they all talked of the sickness of the land, of the broken tribe and the broken house, of young men and young girls who went away and forgot their customs, and lived loose and idle lives. They talked of criminals, of how white Johannesburg was afraid of black crime. One of them went and got him a newspaper, the *Johannesburg Mail*, and showed him in bold black letters:

OLD COUPLE ROBBED AND BEATEN IN LONELY HOUSE.
FOUR NATIVES ARRESTED.

"That happens nearly every day," he said. "And it is not only the Europeans who are afraid. We are also afraid right here in Sophiatown. It was not long ago that a gang of these youths attacked one of our own African girls: they took her bag, and her money, and would have done worse to her too, but people came running out of the houses."

"You will learn much here in Johannesburg," said the rosy-cheeked priest. "It is not only in your place that there is destruction. But we must talk again."

Msimangu took Kumalo to his own room, and when they had sat themselves down, Kumalo said to him, "You will pardon me if I am hasty, but I am anxious to hear about my sister."

"Yes, yes," said Msimangu. "I am sure you are anxious. You must think I am thoughtless. But you will pardon me if I ask you first, why did she come to Johannesburg?"

"She came to look for her husband, who was recruited for the mines. But when his time was up, he did not return, nor did he write at all. She did not know if he were dead perhaps. So she took her small child and went to look for him." Then because Msimangu did not speak, he asked anxiously, "Is she very sick?"

Msimangu said gravely, "Yes, she is very sick. But it is not that kind of sickness. It is another, a worse kind of sickness. I sent for you firstly because she is a woman that is alone, and secondly because her brother is a priest. I do not know if she ever found her husband, but she has no husband now. It would be truer to say that she has many husbands."

Kumalo said, "My God, oh my God."

"She lives in Claremont, not far from here. It is one of the worst places in Johannesburg. After the police have been there, you can see the liquor running in the streets. You can smell it, you can smell nothing else, wherever you go in that place. This is bad liquor here, made strong with all manner of things that our people have never used. And that is her work, she makes and sells it. I shall hide nothing from you, though it is painful for me. These women sleep with any man for their price. A man has been killed at her place. They gamble and drink and fight. She has been in prison more than once."

He leant back in his chair and moved a book forward and backward on the table. "This is terrible news for you," he said.

Kumalo nodded dumbly. At last Kumalo said, "Where is the child?"

"The child is there. But it is no place for a child. And that too is why I sent for you. Perhaps if you cannot save the mother, you can save the child."

"Where is this place?"

"It is not far from here. I shall take you to-morrow."

"I have another great sorrow." But then he tried to speak and could not, so Msimangu said to him, "Take your time, my brother."

"It is not easy. It is our greatest sorrow."

"A son, maybe? Or a daughter?"

"It is a son. Absalom was his name. He too went away, to look for my sister, but he never returned, nor after a while did he write any more. Our letters, his mother's and mine, all came back to us. And now after what you tell me, I am still more afraid."

"We shall try to find him, my brother. Perhaps your sister will know. You are tired, and I should take you to the room I have got for you."

They rose, and Kumalo said, "It is my habit to pray in the church. Maybe you will show me."

"It is on the way."

Kumalo said humbly, "Maybe you will pray for me."

"I shall do it gladly. My brother, I have of course my work to do, but so long as you are here, my hands are yours."

"You are kind."

Something in the humble voice must have touched Msimangu, for he said, "I am not kind. I am a selfish man, but God put his hands on me, that is all." He picked up Kumalo's bag, but before they reached the door Kumalo stopped him.

"I have one more thing to tell you. I have a brother also, here in Johannesburg. He too does not write any more. John Kumalo, a carpenter."

Msimangu smiled. "I know him," he said. "He is too busy to write. He is one of our great politicians."

"A politician? My brother?"

"Yes, he is a great man in politics." Msimangu paused. "I hope I shall not hurt you further. Your brother has no use for the Church any more. He says that what God has not done for South Africa, man must do. That is what he says."

"This is a bitter journey."

"I can believe it."

"Sometimes I fear—what will the Bishop say when he hears? One of his priests. . . ."

"What can a Bishop say? Something is happening that no Bishop can stop. Who can stop these things from happening? They must go on."

"How can you say so? How can you say they must go on?"

"They must go on," said Msimangu gravely. "You cannot stop the world from going on. My friend, I am a Christian. It is not in my heart to hate the white man. It was a white man who brought my father out of darkness. But you will pardon me if I talk frankly to you. The tragedy is not that things are broken. The tragedy is that they are not mended again. The white man has broken the tribe. And it is my belief that it cannot be mended again. But the house that is broken, and the man that falls apart when the house is broken, these are the tragic things. That is why children break the law, and old white people are robbed and beaten."

He passed his hand across his brow. "It suited the white man to break the tribe. But it has not suited him to build something in the place of what is broken. I have pondered this for many hours and must speak it, for it is the truth for me. They are not all so. There are some white men who give their lives to build up what is broken. But they are not enough. They are afraid, that is the truth. It is fear that rules this land."

He laughed apologetically. "These things are too many to talk about now. They are things to talk over quietly and patiently. You must get Father Vincent to talk about them. He is a white man and can say what must be said. He is the one with the boy's cheeks, the one who wants to hear more about your country."

"I remember him."

.   .   .   .

"Mrs. Lithebe, I bring my friend to you. The Reverend Stephen Kumalo."

"Umfundisi, you are welcome. The room is small, but clean."

"Good night, my brother. Shall I see you in the church to-morrow at seven?"

"Yes, indeed."

"Stay well, my friend. Stay well, Mrs. Lithebe."

"Go well, my friend."

"Go well, umfundisi."

She took him to the small, clean room and lit a candle for him. "Sleep well, umfundisi."

"Sleep well, mother."

He stood a moment in the room. Forty-eight hours ago

he and his wife had been packing his bag in far-away
Ndotsheni. Twenty-four hours ago the train had been
thundering through an unseen country. And now outside,
the movement of people, but behind them, through them,
one could hear the roar of a great city. Johannesburg,
Johannesburg.

Who could believe it?

6

It is not far to Claremont. They lie together: Sophiatown, where anyone may own property, the Western Native
Township, and Claremont, the rubbish-heap of the proud
city. These three lie between two European districts.

So they walked till they came to Claremont and Kumalo
was shocked by its shabbiness and dirtiness, and the close-
ness of the houses, and the dirt in the streets.

"Do you see that woman, my friend? She is one of
the liquor sellers. They say she is one of the richest of our
people in Johannesburg."

"And these children?" asked Kumalo. "Why are they
not at school?"

"Some because they do not care, and some because their
parents do not care, but many because the schools are full.
But here is the house. Do you go in alone?"

"It would be better."

"When you are ready, you will find me next door. There
is a woman of our church there, a good woman who tries
with her husband to bring up good children. But it is hard
in this place."

Kumalo stands alone before the door. There is laughter
in the house, the kind of laughter of which one is afraid.
Perhaps because one is afraid already, perhaps because it is

in truth bad laughter. A woman's voice, and men's voices. But he knocks, and she opens.

"It is I, my sister."

Have no doubt it is fear in her eyes. She draws back a step, and makes no move towards him. She turns and says something that he cannot hear. Chairs are moved, and other things are taken. She turns to him. "I am making ready, my brother."

They stand and look at each other, he anxious, she afraid. She turns and looks back into the room. A door closes, and she says, "Come in, my brother."

Only then does she reach out her hand to him. It is cold and wet, there is no life in it. They sit down, she is silent upon her chair.

"I have come," he said.

"It is good."

"You did not write."

"No, I did not write."

"Where is your husband?"

"I have not found him, my brother."

"But you did not write."

"That is true, indeed."

"Did you not know we were anxious?"

"I had no money to write."

"Not two pennies for a stamp?"

She does not answer him. She does not look at him.

"But I hear you are rich."

"I am not rich."

"I hear you have been in prison."

"That is true, indeed."

"Was it for liquor?"

A spark of life comes into her. She must do something, she cannot keep so silent. She tells him she was not guilty. There was some other woman.

" You stayed with this woman? "

" Yes."

" Why did you stay with such a woman? "

" I had no other place."

" And you helped her with her trade? "

" I had to have money for the child."

" Where is the child? "

She looks round vaguely. She gets up and goes to the yard. She calls, but the voice that was once so sweet has a new quality in it, the quality of the laughter that he heard in the house. She is revealing herself to him.

" I have sent for the child," she says.

" Where is it? "

" It shall be fetched," she says. There is discomfort in her eyes. The anger rises up in him.

" Where shall I sleep? " he asks.

The fear in her eyes is unmistakable. Now she will reveal herself, but his anger masters him, and he does not wait for it.

" You have shamed us," he says in a low voice. " A liquor seller, a prostitute, with a child and you do not know where it is. Your brother a priest. How could you do this to us? "

She looks at him sullenly, like an animal that is tormented.

" I have come to take you back." She falls on the floor and cries; her cries become louder and louder, she has no shame.

" They will hear us," he says, and she tries to control her sobs.

" Do you wish to come back? "

She nods her head. " I do not like Johannesburg," she says. " I am sick here. The child is sick also."

" Do you wish with your heart to come back? "

She nods her head again. She sobs too. "I do not like Johannesburg," she says. She looks at him with eyes of distress and his heart beats faster with hope. "I am a bad woman, my brother. I am no woman to go back."

His eyes fill with tears, his deep gentleness returns to him.

"God forgives us," he says. "Who am I not to forgive? Let us pray." They knelt down, and he prayed. Then peacefully they sat hand in hand.

"And now I ask for your help," he said. "Our child, have you not heard of him?"

"I did hear of him, brother. He was working at some big place in Johannesburg, and he lived in Sophiatown, but where, I am not sure. But I know who will know. The son of our brother John and your son were often together. He will know."

"I shall go there. And now, my sister, I must see if Mrs. Lithebe has a room for you. Have you many things?"

"Not many. This table and those chairs, and a bed. And some few dishes and pots. That is all."

"I shall find someone to fetch them. You will be ready?"

"My brother, here is the child."

Into the room came his little nephew. His clothes were dirty and his nose was dirty, and he put his finger in his mouth, and gazed at his uncle out of wide, saucer-like eyes. Kumalo lifted him up, and wiped his nose clean, and kissed him.

"It will be better for the child," he said. "He will go to a place where the wind blows, and where there is a school for him."

"It will be better," she agreed.

"I must go," he said. "There is much to do."

* * * * * * * *

He fetched her with a lorry that afternoon, while a crowd

of interested neighbours discussed the affair loudly and
frankly, some with approval, and some with the strange
laughter of the towns. He was glad when the lorry was
loaded and they left.

Mrs. Lithebe showed them their room, and gave the
mother and child their food. And that night they held
prayers in the dining-room, Kumalo, Mrs. Lithebe and
Gertrude. Kumalo himself was light-hearted and gay like
a boy, more so than he had been for years. One day in
Johannesburg, and already the tribe was being rebuilt, the
house and the soul restored.

7

Gertrude's dress, for all that she might once have been
rich, was dirty, and made him ashamed. Although his
money was little, he bought her a red dress; also a shirt and
a pair of short trousers for the boy. In his pocket was his
Post Office Book, and there was ten pounds there that he
and his wife were saving to buy the stove, for that, like any
other woman, she had long been wanting to have. To save
ten pounds from a salary of eight pounds a month takes
much patience and time, especially for a priest, who must
dress in good black clothes. It was a pity about the ten
pounds, but it would sooner or later have to be broken
into. Strange that she had saved nothing from her sad
employment, which brought in much money, it was said.

Gertrude was helping Mrs. Lithebe in the house, and he
could hear her singing a little. The small boy was playing
in the yard. The sun was shining, and even in this great
city there were birds singing. But there was Msimangu
coming up the street, so Kumalo put aside the letter he was
writing to his wife.

" Are you ready, my friend? "

" Yes, I am ready."

They walked up the street, and down another, and up yet another. It was true what they said, that you could go up one street and down another till the end of your days, and never walk the same one twice.

" Here is your brother's shop. You see his name. Shall I come with you? "

" Yes, I think it would be right."

His brother John was sitting there on a chair, talking to two other men. He had grown fat, and sat with his hands on his knees like a chief. His brother he did not recognize, for the light from the street was on the backs of his visitors.

" Good morning, my brother."

" Good morning, sir."

" Good morning, my own brother, son of our mother."

John Kumalo looked closely at him, and stood up with a great hearty smile.

" My own brother. Well, well, who can believe! What are you doing in Johannesburg? "

Kumalo looked at the visitors. "I came on business," he said.

" I am sure my friends will excuse us." The two men rose and they all said stay well and go well.

" Do you know the Reverend Msimangu, my brother? "

" Well, well, everybody knows the Reverend Msimangu. Sit down, gentlemen. I think we must have some tea." He went to the door and called into the place behind.

" Is your wife Esther well, my brother? "

John Kumalo smiled his jolly, knowing smile. "My wife Esther has left me ten years, my brother."

" And have you married again? "

" Well, well, not what the Church calls married, you know. But she is a good woman."

"You wrote nothing of this, brother."

"No, how could I write? You people in Ndotsheni do not understand the way life is in Johannesburg. I thought it better not to write."

"But I do not understand. How is life different in Johannesburg?"

"Well, that is difficult. Do you mind if I speak in English? I can explain these things better in English."

"Speak in English, then, brother."

"You see I have had an experience here in Johannesburg. It is not like Ndotsheni. One must live here to understand it." He looked at his brother. "Something new is happening here," he said. He did not sit down, but began to speak in a strange voice, and he walked about.

"Down in Ndotsheni I am nobody, even as you are nobody, my brother. I am subject to the chief, who is an ignorant man. I must bow to him, but he is an uneducated man. Here in Johannesburg I am a man of some importance, of some influence. I have my own business, and when it is good, I can make ten, twelve pounds a week." He began to sway to and fro; he was not speaking to them, he was speaking to people who were not there. "I do not say we are free here. I do not say we are free as men should be. But at least I am free of the chief. At least I am free of an old and ignorant man, who is nothing but a white man's dog. He is a trick, a trick to hold together something that the white man desires to hold together."

He smiled his cunning and knowing smile, and for a moment addressed himself to his visitors. "But it is not being held together," he said. "It is breaking apart, your tribal society. It is here in Johannesburg that the new society is being built. Something is happening here, my brother."

He paused for a moment, then he said, "I do not wish to

offend you, gentleman, but the Church too is like the chief. You must do so and so and so. You are not free to have an experience. A man must be faithful and obedient, and he must obey the laws, whatever the laws may be. It is true that the Church speaks with a fine voice, and that the Bishops speak against the laws. But this they have been doing for fifty years, and things get worse, not better."

His voice grew louder, and he was again addressing people who were not there. "Here in Johannesburg it is the mines," he said, "everything is the mines. These high buildings, this beautiful city with its beautiful houses, all this is built with the gold from the mines. This wonderful hospital for Europeans is built with the gold from the mines."

There was a change in his voice, it became louder like the voice of a bull or a lion. "Go to our hospital," he said, "and see our people lying on the floors. They lie so close you cannot step over them. But it is they who dig the gold. For three shillings a day. We come from our tribes, from all over South Africa. We live in the compounds, we must leave our wives and families behind. And when the new gold is found, it is not we who will get more for our labour. It is the white man's shares that will rise. They go mad when new gold is found. They bring more of us to live in the compounds, to dig under the ground for three shillings a day. They do not think, here is a chance to pay more for our labour. They think only, here is a chance to build a bigger house and buy a bigger car. It is important to find gold, they say, for all South Africa is built on the mines."

He growled and his voice grew deep, it was like thunder that was rolling. "But it is not built on the mines," he said, "it is built on our backs, on our sweat, on our labour.

Every factory, every theatre, every beautiful house, they are built by us. And what does a chief know about that? But here in Johannesburg they know."

He stopped, and was silent. And his visitors were silent also, for there was something in this voice that compelled one to be silent. And Stephen Kumalo sat silent, for this was a new brother that he saw.

John Kumalo looked at him. "The Bishop says it is wrong," he said, "but he lives in a big house, and his white priests get four, five, six times what you get, my brother." He sat down, and took out a large red handkerchief to wipe his face. "That is my experience," he said "That is why I no longer go to the church."

"And that is why you did not write any more?"

"Well, well, it could be the reason."

"That, and your wife Esther?"

"Yes, yes, both perhaps. It is hard to explain in a letter. Our customs are different here."

And Msimangu said, "Are there any customs here?"

John Kumalo looked at him. "There is a new thing growing here," he said. "Stronger than any church or chief. You will see it one day."

"And your wife? Why did she leave?"

"Well, well," said John Kumalo with his knowing smile. "She did not understand my experience."

"You mean," said Msimangu coldly, "that she believed in being faithful."

John looked at him suspiciously. "Faithful?" he said. The angry veins stood out on the great bull neck, and who knows what angry words might have been spoken, but Stephen Kumalo was quick to intervene. "Here is the tea, my brother. That is kind of you."

The woman was not introduced, but took round the tea humbly. When she had gone, Kumalo spoke to his brother.

"I have listened attentively to you. Much of what you say saddens me, partly because of the way you say it, and partly because much of it is true. And now I have something to ask you. But I must tell you first that Gertrude is with me here. She is coming back to Ndotsheni."

"Well, well, I shall not say it is a bad thing. Johannesburg is not a place for a woman alone. I myself tried to persuade her, but she did not agree, so we did not meet any more."

"And now I must ask you, where is my son?"

There is something like discomfort in John's eyes. He takes out his handkerchief again. "Well, you have heard, no doubt, he was friendly with my son. Well, you know how these young men are. You see, my son did not agree well with his second mother. Many times I tried to arrange matters, but I did not succeed. So he said he would leave. He had good work, so I did not stop him. And your son went with him."

"Where, my brother?"

"I do not rightly know. But I heard that they had a room in Alexandra. Now wait a minute. They were both working for a factory. I remember. The Doornfontein Company, in Krause Street."

They said their farewells and went out into the street.

"Huh, there you have it," said Msimangu. "He is a big man, in this place, your brother. His shop is always full of men, talking as you have heard. But they say you must hear him at a meeting, he and Dubala. They say he speaks like a bull, and growls in his throat like a lion, and could make men mad if he would. But for that they say he has not enough courage, for he would surely be sent to prison. I shall tell you one thing," Msimangu continued. "Because the white man has power, we too want power. But I see only one hope for our country, and that is when white men and black men, desiring neither power nor money, but desiring only the good of their country, come together to work for it. And I have one great fear in my heart, that one day when the white man has turned to loving, he will find we have turned to hating. But this is not the way to get to Doornfontein," he said. "Come, let us hurry."

.   .   .   .

But they were not successful at Doornfontein, although the white men treated them with consideration and said that when Absalom Kumalo left the factory some twelve months before, he was staying with a Mrs. Ndela at 105 End Street, Sophiatown.

So they returned to Sophiatown, and indeed found Mrs. Ndela at 105 End Street. But Absalom was not there, she said. But wait, she had had a letter from him, asking about the things he had left behind. And while she was searching in a box of papers for the letter, Msimangu saw her stop in her search for a moment, and look at Kumalo, half curiously, and half with pity. At last she found the letter, and she showed them the address; with a Mrs. Mkize, 79 Twenty-Third Avenue, Alexandra.

Then they must drink a cup of tea, and it was dark before they rose to leave, and the husband stepped out with Kumalo into the street.

"Why did you look at my friend with pity?" asked Msimangu of the woman. She dropped her eyes, then raised them again. "He is an umfundisi," she said. "I did not like his son's friends. Nor did my husband. That is why he left us."

"I understand you. Was there anything worse than that?"

"No, I saw nothing. But I did not like his friends."

"Good night, mother."

"Good night, umfundisi."

Out in the street they said farewell to the husband, and set off back to the Mission House. "To-morrow," said Msimangu, "we go to Alexandra."

Kumalo put his hand on his friend's arm. "The things are not happy that brought me to Johannesburg," he said, "but I have found much pleasure in your company."

"Huh," said Msimangu. "Huh. We must hurry or we shall be late for our food."

8

The next morning Msimangu and Kumalo took a bus which set them down at the place where Kumalo had lost his pound. Then they walked to the bus rank for Alexandra. But here they met an unexpected obstacle, for a young man came up to them and said to Msimangu, "Are you going to Alexandra, umfundisi?"

"Yes, my friend."

"We are here to stop you, umfundisi. Not by force, you see"—he pointed—"the police are there to prevent that. But by persuasion. If you use this bus you are weakening the cause of the black people. We have determined not to use these buses until the fare is brought back again to fourpence."

"Yes, indeed, I have heard of it." He turned to Kumalo. "I was very foolish. I had forgotten that there were no buses; at least I had forgotten the boycott of the buses."

"Our business is very urgent," said Kumalo humbly.

"Our boycott is also urgent," said the man politely. "They want us to pay sixpence, that is one shilling a day.

Six shillings a week, and some of us only get thirty-five or forty shillings."

" Is it far to walk? " asked Kumalo.

" It is a long way, umfundisi. Eleven miles."

" That is a long way, for an old man."

" Men as old as you are doing it every day, umfundisi. And women, and some that are sick, and children. They start walking at four in the morning, and they do not get back till eight at night. They have a little food, and their eyes are hardly closed on the pillow before they must stand up again, sometimes to start off again with nothing but hot water in their stomachs. I cannot stop you taking a bus, umfundisi, but this is a cause to fight for. If we lose it, then they will have to pay more in Sophiatown and other places."

" I understand you well. We shall not use the bus." The man thanked them and went to another traveller to persuade him.

" That man has a silver tongue," said Kumalo.

" That is the famous Dubala, a friend of your brother John. But they say your brother has the voice, but that this man has the heart. He is the one the Government is afraid of, because he himself is not afraid. He seeks nothing for himself. They say he has given up his own work to do this, and his wife does the other bus rank at Alexandra."

" That is something to be proud of. Johannesburg is a place of wonders."

" They were church people, but are so no longer. Like your brother, they say the Church has a fine voice, but no deeds. Well, my friend, what do we do now? "

" I am willing to walk."

" Eleven miles, and eleven miles back. It is a long journey."

"I am willing. You understand I am anxious. This Johannesburg—it is no place for a boy to be alone."

"Good. Let us begin then." So they walked many miles through the city. After a long time a car stopped and a white man spoke to them. "Where are you two going?" he asked.

"To Alexandra, sir," said Msimangu, taking off his hat.

"I thought you might be. Climb in." That was a great help to them, and at the turn to Alexandra they got out and expressed their thanks. "It is a long journey," said the white man. "And I know that you have no buses." They stood to watch him go on, but he did not go on. He turned his car round, and was soon on the road back to Johannesburg.

"Huh," said Msimangu, "that is something to marvel at."

It was still a long way to Twenty-third Avenue, and as they passed one avenue after the other, Msimangu explained that Alexandra was outside the boundaries of Johannesburg, and was a place where a black man could buy land and own a house. But the streets were not cared for, and there were no lights, and so great was the demand for houses that every man, if he could, built rooms in his yard and let them to others. Many of these rooms were the hiding-places of thieves, and there was much prostitution and making of liquor.

At last they came to the house they were looking for. A woman opened the door to them. She gave them no greeting, and when they stated their business, she let them in unwillingly.

"You say the boy has gone, Mrs. Mkize?"

"Yes, I do not know where he is gone."

"When did he go?"

" These many months. A year it must be."

" And had he a friend? "

" Yes, another Kumalo. The son of his father's brother. But they left together."

" And you do not know where they went? "

" They talked of many places. But you know how these young men talk."

" How did he behave himself, this young man Absalom? " Kumalo asked her. Have no doubt it is fear in her eyes. Have no doubt it is fear now in his eyes also. It is fear, here in this house. " I saw nothing wrong," she said.

" Then why are you afraid? "

" I am not afraid," she said.

" Then why do you tremble? " asked Msimangu.

" I am cold," she said. She looked at them sullenly, watchfully. " We thank you," said Msimangu. " Stay well."

" Go well," she said.

Out in the street Kumalo spoke. " There is something wrong."

" I do not deny it. My friend, two of us are too many together. Turn left at the big street and wait for me there." Heavy-hearted the old man went, and Msimangu returned to the house. She opened again to him, as sullen as before. " I am not from the police," he said. " I have nothing to do with the police; I wish to have nothing to do with them. But there is an old man suffering because he cannot find his son."

" That is a bad thing," she said, but she spoke just words, not her feelings.

" It is a bad thing," he said, " and I cannot leave you until you have told me what you would not tell."

" I have nothing to tell," she said.

"You have nothing to tell because you are afraid. And you do not tremble because it is cold."

"And why do I tremble?" she asked.

"That I do not know. But I shall not leave you till I discover it. And if it is necessary I shall go to the police after all, because there will be no other place to go."

"It is hard for a woman who is alone," she said.

"It is hard for an old man seeking his son."

"I am afraid," she said.

"He is afraid also. Could you not see he is afraid?"

"I could see it, umfundisi."

"Then tell me, what sort of a life did they lead here, these two young men?" But she kept silent, with the fear in her eyes. He could see that she would be hard to move. "I am a priest. Would you not take my word?" But she kept silent. "Have you a Bible? I will swear to you on the Bible." But she kept silent till he said again, "I will swear to you on the Bible." So getting no peace, she went to a room behind, and returned with the Bible.

"I am a priest," he said. "My yes has always been yes, and my no, no. But because you desire it, and because an old man is afraid, I swear to you on this Book that no trouble will come to you of this, for we seek only a boy. What sort of a life did they lead?"

"They brought many things here, umfundisi, in the late hours of the night. They were clothes, and watches, and money, and food in bottles, and many other things."

"Was there ever blood on them?"

"I never saw blood on them, umfundisi."

"That is something. Only a little, but something. And why did they leave."

"I do not know, umfundisi. But I think they were near to being discovered."

"And they left about a year ago? And you do not know where they are gone?"

"No, but they were friendly with the taxi-driver Hlabeni. Near the bus rank he lives. Everyone knows him."

"For that I give you thanks. Stay well, Mrs. Mkize."

He met Kumalo at the corner, and they soon found Hlabeni the taxi-driver, sitting in his taxi. "Good afternoon, my friend," said Msimangu.

"Good afternoon, umfundisi."

"I want a taxi, my friend. What do you charge to Johannesburg?"

"For you, umfundisi, I should charge eleven shillings."

"It is a lot of money."

"Another taxi would charge you fifteen or twenty shillings."

The man was about to start his engine, but Msimangu said, "I am told that you can help me to find a young man, Absalom Kumalo." Have no doubt too, that this man is afraid. But Msimangu is quick to reassure him. "I am not here for trouble," he said. "But my companion is the father of this young man, and he has come from Natal to find him."

"Yes, I knew this young man."

"And where is he now, my friend?"

"I heard he was gone to live in Shanty Town."

"There you have helped me, my friend. Come, we shall take your taxi." They climbed in, and the taxi rattled out of Alexandra on to the broad high-road. "You see the bicycles. These are the thousands of Alexandra people returning home after their work, and soon we shall see thousands of them walking, because of the boycott of the buses." And true, they had not gone far before the pavements were full of the walking people. Many of the white people stopped their cars, and took in the black people, to help them on their journey to Alexandra. They saw the police trying to prevent this, and once when they stopped they heard one policeman ask a white man if he had a licence to carry the black people. "I am asking no money," said the white man. "But you are carrying passengers on a bus route," said the officer. "Then take me to court," said the white man. But they heard no more than that, for they had to move on with the traffic.

"Then take me to court," repeated Msimangu quietly. "Then take me to court."

9

All roads lead to Johannesburg. If you are white or if you are black they lead to Johannesburg. If the crops fail, there is work in Johannesburg. If there are taxes to be paid, there is work in Johannesburg. If the farm is too small to be divided further, some must go to Johannesburg. If there is a child to be born that must be born in secret, it can be born in Johannesburg.

The black people go to Alexandra, or Sophiatown, or Orlando, and try to hire rooms, or to buy a share of a house.

"Have you a room that you could let?"

"No, I have no room."

"Have you a room that you could let?"

"It is let already."

"Have you a room that you could let?" . . .

.   .   .   .

"They say there are ten thousand of us in Orlando alone, living in other people's houses."

"Do you hear what Dubala says? That we must put up our own houses here in Orlando?"

" And where do we put up the houses? "

" On the open ground by the railway line, Dubala says."

" And of what do we build the houses? "

" Anything you can find. Sacks and planks and grass from the veld and poles from the fields."

" And when it rains? "

" When it rains, they will have to build us houses."

" It is foolishness. What shall we do in the winter? "

Six years waiting for a house. And the houses grow yet fuller, for the people still come to Johannesburg. There has been a great war in Europe and North Africa, and no houses are being built.

.   .   .   .

This night they are busy in Orlando. " I shall carry the iron, and you, my wife, the child, and you, my son, two poles and many sacks, down to the land by the railway lines." Many people are moving there, you can hear the sound of digging and hammering already. It is good that the night is warm, and there is no rain. " Thank you, Mr. Dubala, we are satisfied with this piece of ground. Thank you, Mr. Dubala, here is our shilling for the Committee."

Shanty Town is up overnight. What a surprise for the people when they wake in the morning. Shanty Town is up overnight. And the newspapers are full of us. This great village of sack and plank and iron, with no rent to pay, only a shilling to the Committee. Shanty Town is up overnight. The child coughs badly, and her brow is as hot as fire. The cold wind comes through the sacks. " What shall we do in the rain, in the winter? Quietly, my child, do not cough any more, your mother is by you." But the child coughs badly, her brow is hotter than fire.

" What shall we do in the rain? in the winter? " Already some of them are saying, " Look at those houses over the hill which they have started to build because we built Shanty Town. They are not finished, but the roofs are on. One night we shall move there and be safe from the rain and the winter."

10

"And this is Shanty Town, my friend." Kumalo looked around at the tragic houses. A sheet of iron, a few planks, sacks and grass, an old door from some forgotten house. There is a smell of food, there is a sound of voices. The sun shines warmly down from the cloudless sky. But what will they do when it rains, what will they do when it is winter?

"See, there is one of our black nurses. Does she not look well in her uniform? The white people are training more and more of them. It is strange how we move forward in some things, and go backward in others. Yet in this matter of nurses and doctors we have many friends among the white people. Good morning, nurse. Did you ever know a young man, Absalom Kumalo?"

"Yes, I did. But he is not here now. He stayed at that house over there."

The woman of the house smiled at them in a friendly way. "Mother, we are looking for a lad, Absalom Kumalo."

"He stayed with me, umfundisi. We took pity on him because he had no place to go. But I am sorry to tell you that they took him away, and the magistrate sent him to the reformatory."

"The reformatory?"

"Yes, the big school beyond the hospital. It is not too far to walk."

"I must thank you, mother. Stay well. Come, my friend." They walked on in silence, for neither of them had any words. Kumalo would have stumbled, though the road was straight and even, and Msimangu took his arm. "Have courage, my brother."

"Sometimes it seems that I have no more courage. I was afraid of this."

"Yes, I too was afraid of it."

"Yes, I remember when you first became afraid. The day at Alexandra, when you sent me on, and you returned to speak again to the woman. What did the woman say to you, my friend?"

"She said that these two young men were in some mischief. Many goods, white people's goods, came to the house."

"This reformatory, can they reform there?"

"I do not know. Some people say one thing, some the other. But your friend the priest from England speaks well of it."

They came to the reformatory where one of their own people, a pleasant fellow, asked them what they wanted, and took them to an office where a young white man inquired of them in Afrikaans what was their business.

"We are looking, sir, for the son of my friend, one Absalom Kumalo," said Msimangu in the same language.

"Absalom Kumalo. Yes, I know him well. Strange, he told me he had no people."

"Your son told him that he had no people," said Msimangu in Zulu. "He was no doubt ashamed," said Kumalo. "I am sorry," he said to Msimangu in Zulu, "that I speak no Afrikaans." For he had heard that sometimes they do not like black people who speak no Afrikaans. The young man understood him and said in English, "You may speak what you will. Your son did well here and I have great hope for his future."

" You mean, sir, that he is gone? "

"Gone, yes, only one month ago. We made an exception in his case, partly because of his good behaviour, partly because of his age, but mainly because there was a girl who is going to have a child by him. She came here to see him, and he seemed fond of her, and anxious about the child that would be born. And so with his solemn undertaking he would work for his child and its mother, we let him go."

" And is he now married, sir? "

" No, umfundisi, he is not. But everything is arranged for the marriage. This girl has no people, and your son told us he had no people, so I myself have arranged it."

" That is good of you, sir. I thank you for them."

" It is our work. You must not worry too much about this matter, and the fact that they were not married. The real question is whether he will care for them, and lead a decent life. I will take you to Pimville, where Absalom and this girl are living. He will not be there, because I have found work for him in the town, and they have given me good reports of him. I persuaded him to open a Post Office Book, and he already has three or four pounds in it."

" Indeed I cannot thank you, sir."

" It is our work," said the young man.

At the house in Pimville they were greeted by a young girl, who herself seemed no more than a child. " We have come to inquire after Absalom," said the young white man. " This umfundisi is his father."

" He went on Saturday to Springs," she said, " and he has not yet returned." The young man was silent awhile, and he frowned in perplexity or anger. "But this is Tuesday," he said. "Have you heard nothing from him?"

"Nothing," she said.

"When will he return?" he asked

"I do not know," she said.

"Will he ever return?" he asked.

"I do not know," she said. She said it hopelessly, as one who is used to waiting, to desertion. Kumalo was moved to pity.

"What will you do?" he said.

"I do not know," she said.

Msimangu turned to Kumalo. "You can do nothing here," he said. "Let us go. Have you not troubles enough of your own? I tell you there are thousands of such girls in Johannesburg."

"You do not understand. The child will be my grand-child."

"Even that you do not know," said Msimangu angrily. "And if he were, how many such more have you? Shall we search them out, day after day, hour after hour? Will it ever end?"

Kumalo stood in the dust like one who has been struck. Then without speaking any more he took his seat in the car. They stopped at the gate of the village, and the young white man got out and went into an office. He came back, his face unhappy. "I have telephoned the factory," he said. "It is true. He has not been at work this week." At Orlando they climbed out, and the young man spoke to Kumalo. "I am sorry for this," he said.

"I am sorry too, for this end to your work."

"Yes, it is my work, but it is your son. Let us not give up all hope. It has happened sometimes that a boy is arrested, or is injured and taken to hospital, and we do not know. Do not give up hope, umfundisi. I will not give up the search."

They watched him drive away. "He is a good man," said Kumalo. "Come, let us walk." But Msimangu did not move. "I am ashamed to walk with you," he said. "I ask your forgiveness for my ugly words."

"You are forgiven. But I have something to ask of you." Msimangu looked at him, searching his face, and then he said, "It is agreed."

"What is agreed?"

"That I should take you again to see this girl." They walked along the hot road to Orlando, and both fell silent, each, no doubt, with many things in mind.

II

It was a pleasant evening at the Mission House. Father Vincent, the rosy-cheeked priest, was there, and they talked about the place where Kumalo lived and worked. And the white man, in his turn, spoke about his own country. Yet even this pleasure was not to be entire, for one of the white priests came in from the city with the evening newspaper, and showed them the bold, black lines.

MURDER IN PARKWOLD. WELL-KNOWN CITY ENGINEER
SHOT DEAD. ATTACKERS THOUGHT TO BE NATIVES.

"This is a terrible loss for South Africa," said the white priest. "For this Arthur Jarvis was a courageous young man, and a great fighter for justice. And it is a terrible loss for the Church too. He was one of the finest of all our young helpers, and was the President of the African Boys' Club, here in Claremont."

"Perhaps you might have known him," said Father

Vincent to Kumalo. "It says that he was the only child of Mr. James Jarvis, of High Place, Carisbrooke."

"I know the father," said Kumalo sorrowfully. "I mean I know him well by sight and name, but we have never spoken. His farm is in the hills above Ndotsheni, and he sometimes rode past our church. But I did not know the son." He was silent, then he said, "Yet I remember, there was a small, bright boy, and he too sometimes rode on his horse past the church. A small, bright boy, I remember, though I do not remember it well." And he was silent again, for who is not silent when someone is dead, who was a small, bright boy?

"Shall I read this?" said Father Vincent.

"'At 1.30 p.m. to-day, Mr. Jarvis, of Plantation Road, Parkwold, was shot dead in his house by someone thought to be a native. Mrs. Jarvis and her two children were away, and Mr. Jarvis had stayed at home with a slight cold. It would seem that a native, probably with two companions, entered by the kitchen, thinking, no doubt, that there would be no one in the house. The native servant in the kitchen was knocked unconscious, and it would appear that Mr. Jarvis heard the disturbance and came down to investigate. He was shot dead at short range.

"Three native youths were seen waiting in Plantation Road shortly before the tragedy occurred. The native servant is lying unconscious in the Non-European Hospital, and it is hoped that when he regains consciousness he will be able to give the police important information. His condition is serious, however.

"The dead man was well known for the welfare of the non-European sections of the community.'"

A silence falls upon them all. This is no time to talk of the beauties of any country. Sadness and fear and hate, how they rise up in the heart and mind! Cry for the broken

tribe, for the law and custom that is gone. And cry aloud
for the man who is dead, for the woman and children who
have lost him. Cry, the beloved country, these things are
not yet at an end. The sun pours down on the earth, on
the lovely land that man cannot enjoy. He knows only the
fear of his heart.

.   .   .   .

Msimangu walked with Kumalo to the gate of the little
house of Mrs. Lithebe. Kumalo's face was full of suffering.
"This thing," he said. "This thing. Here in my heart
there is nothing but fear. Fear, fear, fear."

"I understand. Yet it is foolish to fear that one thing in
this great city, with its thousands and thousands of people."

"It is not a question of wisdom and foolishness. It is
just fear."

"Come and pray."

"There is no prayer left in me. I am dumb here inside.
I have no words at all."

"Good night, my brother."

"Good night."

There are times, no doubt, when God seems no more to
be about the world.

12

Have no doubt it is fear in the land. For what can men
do when so many have grown lawless? Who can enjoy the
lovely land, who can enjoy the seventy years, and the sun
that pours down on the earth, when there is fear in the
heart? Who can walk quietly in the shadow of the trees,
when there is danger? Who can lie peacefully in bed,
while the darkness holds some secret?

There are voices crying what must be done; a hundred, a thousand voices. But what do they help if one cries this, and one cries that, and another cries something that is neither this nor that.

It's a scandal that we have so few police. We must demand more protection. . . .

I say we shall always have native crime to fear until the native people of this country have worthy purposes and worthy goals to work for. It is only because they see neither purpose nor goal that they turn to drink and crime and prostitution. The answer does not lie in more police and more protection. . . . .

I am sure that increased schooling would cause a decrease in crime amongst native children.

Don't you think that more schooling would only produce cleverer criminals? . . .

Why can't they make recreation places for the natives, away from the European districts?

And how long will it take them to get there? And how long to get back? How many hours do you give your servants off on a Sunday?

Oh, it's too hot to argue. . . .

· · · · · · · ·

Yes, there are a hundred and a thousand voices crying. But what does one do, when one cries this thing, and one cries another? Who knows how we shall create a land of peace where black outnumbers white so greatly?

Cry, the beloved country, for the unborn child that is the inheritor of our fear. Let him not love the earth too deeply. Let him not laugh too gladly when the water runs through his fingers, nor stand too silent when the setting sun makes red the veld with fire. Let him not be too moved when the birds of his land are singing, nor give too much of his heart to a mountain or a valley. For fear will rob him of all if he gives too much.

．　　．　　．　　．　　．　　．　　．　　．

" Mr. Msimangu? "

" Ah, it is Mrs. Ndela of End Street."

" Mr. Msimangu, the police have been to me. They are looking for the son of the old umfundisi."

" For what, mother? "

" They did not say, Mr. Msimangu."

" Is it bad, mother? "

" It looks as if it were bad. I was frightened, umfundisi. So I gave them the address. Mrs. Mkize, 79 Twenty-Third Avenue, Alexandra. And one said, yes, this woman was known to the police. Did I do wrong, umfundisi? I was afraid."

" You did no wrong, mother. It is the law. We must obey the law."

He thanks the simple woman, and tells her to go well. He stands for a moment, then turns swiftly to go out. But he is too late for, as he opens his door, Kumalo stands before him. " You are going out, my friend? " Msimangu is silent.

" Come in," said Msimangu at last, and he shut the door. " I have just had a visit from Mrs. Ndela. The police came to her house looking for the boy. She gave them the address of Mrs. Mkize."

" Why do they want the boy? " asked Kumalo.

" That we do not know. I was ready to go there when you came."

" You were going alone? " the old man asked.

" I was going alone, yes. But now that I have told you, you may come also. There are no buses, so we must go by taxi."

"I have money. No one must pay but me."

"It will take a great deal of money," said Msimangu. Kumalo took out his purse eagerly. "Here is my money," he said.

"We shall use it then. Come, let us look for a taxi."

.   .   .   .

"Mrs. Mkize!" She drew back, hostile. "Have the police been here? What did they want?"

"They wanted the boy."

"And where have they gone?"

"To Shanty Town." She draws back again, remembering.

"To the address you said you did not know," said Msimangu.

"What could I do?" she said. "It was the police. I did not know the address. Shanty Town, I told them."

.   .   .   .

In Shanty Town, at the house they had visited before, Msimangu asked, "Have the police been here?"

"They were here, umfundisi. They wanted the boy."

"For what, mother? Did it seem heavy?"

"I do not know, umfundisi."

"And where have they gone?"

"To the reformatory, umfundisi."

.   .   .   .

At the reformatory the white man was out, and Msimangu asked the native assistant, "Have the police been here?"

"They have been here. It was now, now, that they left. They wanted the boy, Absalom Kumalo."

"Why did they want him? Did it seem heavy?"

"I do not know. I really could not say."

" And where did they go? "

" To Pimville, umfundisi. To the home of the girl."

.   .   .   .

" My child! Have the police been here? "

" They have been here, now, now, they were here. They wanted Absalom, umfundisi. I told them I had not seen him since Saturday."

" And why did they want him? " cried Kumalo in torment.

She drew back frightened. " I do not know," she said.

" Did it seem heavy? " asked Msimangu.

" It seemed heavy, umfundisi. What is the trouble? " she asked.

" We do not know," replied Msimangu.

" The world is full of trouble," she said. " They told me I must let them know if he comes." Her eyes were full of trouble. " What shall I do? " she said.

" Tell the police," said Msimangu, " and tell us also."

.   .   .   .

" How much is your charge? " asks Msimangu.

" Two pounds and ten shillings," says the taxi-driver.

" I should like to help you in this," says Msimangu.

" You are kind," says Kumalo, trembling, " but no one must pay but me." And he draws the notes from the diminishing store.

" You are trembling, my friend."

" I am cold, very cold."

Msimangu looks up at the cloudless sky, from which the sun of Africa is pouring down upon the earth. " Come to my room," he says. " We shall have a fire and make you warm again."

13

That evening, alone in his own room, Kumalo sat and thought. Yes, it was true what Msimangu had said. Why fear the one thing in a great city where there were thousands upon thousands of people? His son had gone astray in the great city, where so many others had gone astray. But that he should kill a man, a white man! There was nothing that he could remember, nothing, nothing at all, in all the years of the boyhood of his son, that could make it possible for him to do so terrible a deed. Perhaps when his son and the girl were married they would go back with him to Ndotsheni, and then he could try to rebuild what had been broken.

Yes, Msimangu was right. It was the not knowing that made him fear this one thing, in a great city where there were thousands upon thousands of people.

14

Two days later, just as Kumalo was about to call the small boy to play with him, he saw, with the fear catching at him suddenly with a physical pain, Msimangu and the young white man coming into the house.

"Good afternoon, umfundisi. Is there a place where we can talk?" asked the young man.

"Come to my room," he said, hardly trusting to his voice. In the room he shut the door, and stood not looking at them.

"I have heard what you fear," said the young man. "It is true." And Kumalo could not look at them. He sat down in his chair and fixed his eyes upon the floor. What does one say now?

" They will say we let him out too soon," said the young man at last. " The other two were not reformatory boys. But it was he who fired the shot."

" My friend," said Msmangu, in as ordinary a voice as he could find, " one of the two others is the son of your brother."

" Do you wish to come to the prison, umfundisi? I have arranged it for you." And Kumalo nodded. " But my brother first," he said.

" I shall show you the way," said Msimangu. " And I shall wait at the Mission," said the young man.

" I shall walk slowly up the street," said Kumalo. " You must tell the women." " I shall tell them, my friend," said Msimangu.

Msimangu caught him up at the top of the hill, and took his arm, and it was like walking with a child or with one that was sick. So they came to the shop. " Do not come further," said Kumalo. " It is I who must do this."

Yes, the bull voice was there, loud and confident. His brother John was sitting there on a chair, talking to two other men, sitting there like a chief. " Ah, my brother, it is you. Well, well, I am glad to see you. Will you not come and join us? "

" I am sorry, but I come again on business, urgent business."

" I am sure my friends will excuse us." So they all said stay well, and go well, and the two men left them.

" Well, well, I am glad to see you, my brother. And your business, how does it progress? Have you found the wandering boy? " And he laughed at that, a great bull laugh.

" He is found, my brother. He is in prison, arrested for the murder of a white man."

" Murder? " The man does not jest now. One does not

jest about murder. Still less about the murder of a white man.

"Yes, murder. He broke into a house in a place they call Parkwold, and killed the white man who would have prevented him."

"What? I remember! Only a day or two ago? On Tuesday?" Yes, he remembers. He remembers too that his own son and his brother's son are companions. The veins stand out on the bull neck, and the sweat forms on the brow. Have no doubt it is fear in the eyes. He wipes his brow with a cloth.

"I am sorry, my brother," says Kumalo.

"You mean . . . ?"

"Yes. He was there also."

John Kumalo whispers, "God, God." And again, "God. Oh, my God!" Kumalo puts his hand on his brother's shoulders. "There are many things I could say. But I say only that I know what you suffer. There is a young white man waiting to take me to the prison. Perhaps he would take you also."

They set out along the street to the Mission House. The old man walks now more firmly, it is the other who seems bowed and broken.

Father Vincent, the rosy-cheeked priest from England, takes Kumalo's hand in both his own. "Anything," he says, "anything. You have only to ask. I shall do anything."

.   .   .   .

They pass through the great gate in the grim high wall. John Kumalo is taken to one room, and the young man goes with Stephen Kumalo to another. There the son is brought to them. The old man takes his son's hand in both his own, and the hot tears fell fast upon them. The boy stands unhappy, there is no gladness in his eyes. He twists his head from side to side.

"My child, my child."

"Yes, my father."

"At last I have found you."

"Yes, my father."

"And it is too late." To this the boy makes no answer. As though he may find some hope in this silence, the father presses him. "Is it not too late?" he asks. But there is no answer. Almost eagerly, "Is it not too late?" he asks.

"My father, it is what my father says," he answers.

"I have searched in every place for you." To that also no answer. The old man loosens his hands, and his son's hands slip from them lifelessly. "Why did you do this terrible thing?"

"I do not know," he says.

"Why did you carry a revolver?"

"For safety," he says. "This Johannesburg is a dangerous place. A man never knows when he will be attacked."

"But why take it to this house?" And this again cannot be answered.

"Have they got it, my child?"

"Yes, my father."

"They have no doubt it was you?"

"I told them, my father."

"What did you tell them?"

"I told them I was frightened when the white man came. So I shot him. I did not mean to kill him."

"And your cousin? And the other?"

"Yes, I told them. They came with me, but it was I who shot the white man."

"Did you go there to steal?" And this again cannot be answered. "You were at the reformatory, my child? Did they treat you well?"

" They treated me well," he said.

" And this is your repayment, my child? "

The young white man comes over, for he does not like to see these two torturing each other. " Well, Absalom? Why did you leave the work that I got for you? "

And you, young man, can get no answer. There are no answers to these things.

" And your girl. The one we let you go to, the girl who you worried over, so that we took pity on you."

Absalom weeps. Who knows if he weeps for the girl he has deserted? Or does he weep for himself?

" Answer me one thing, my child," says Kumalo. " You wrote nothing, sent no message. You went with bad companions. You stole and broke in. But why? "

The boy seizes upon the word that is given him. " It was bad companions," he says.

" That is no answer," says Kumalo. But he knows he will get no other this way. The young white man comes to them again.

" Do you still wish to marry the girl? " he asks.

" Yes, sir."

" I shall see what I can do," says the young man. " I think it is time for us to go."

" May we come again? "

" Yes, you may come again. We shall ask about it at the gate."

" Stay well, my child."

" Go well, my father."

They go, and outside the gate they meet John Kumalo. He is feeling better, the big bull man. " Well, well," he says, " we must go at once and see a lawyer."

" A lawyer, my brother? For what should we spend such money? The story is plain, there cannot be doubt about it."

" What is the story? " asks John Kumalo.

" The story? These three lads went to a house that they thought was empty. They struck down the servant. The white man heard the noise and he came to see. And then . . . and then . . . my son . . . mine, not yours . . . shot at him. He was afraid, he says."

" Well, well," says John Kumalo, " that is a story. And he told you this in front of the others? "

" Why not, if it is the truth? "

John Kumalo seems reassured. " Perhaps you do not need a lawyer," he said. " If he shot the white man, there is nothing more to be said."

" Will you have a lawyer then? "

John Kumalo smiles at his brother. " Perhaps I shall need a lawyer," he says. " For one thing, a lawyer can talk to my son in private. You see, my brother, there is no proof that my son or this other young man was there at all." Yes, John Kumalo smiles at that, he seems quite recovered.

" Not there at all? But my son . . ."

" Yes, yes," John Kumalo interrupts him, and smiles at him. " Who will believe your son? " he asks. He says it with meaning, with cruel and pitiless meaning. Kumalo looks at his brother, but his brother does not look at him. Indeed, he walks away. Wearily, wearily Kumalo goes from the great gate in the wall to the street. " God," he says, " oh, God, do not leave me." Father Vincent's words come back to him: anything, anything, he said, you have only to ask. Then to Father Vincent he will go.

15

Kumalo returned to Mrs. Lithebe's tired and miserable.

The two women were silent, and he had no desire to play with his small nephew. He withdrew into his room to rest before going to the Mission House, but there was a knock at the door, and there stood the young white man.

"Umfundisi," said the young man, "about this lawyer. I think you must have a lawyer. Not because the truth must not be told, but because I do not trust your brother. You can see what is in his mind. His plan is to deny that his son and the third man were with your son. A lawyer would know whether that will make matters worse or not. And Absalom says that he fired the revolver because he was afraid, with no intention of killing the white man. It needs a lawyer to make the court believe that is true."

"Yes, I see that."

"Do you know of any lawyer, of your Church maybe?"

"No, sir, I do not. But Father Vincent will know."

So they walked to the Mission House.

"I think I could get a good man to take the case," said Father Vincent. "We are agreed that it is to be the truth and nothing but the truth, and that the defence will be that the shot was fired in fear and not to kill."

"And what about the marriage?" asked the young man.

"I shall ask him about that also. I should gladly marry them if it can be arranged." Father Vincent put his hand on the old man's arm. "Be of good courage," he said. "Whatever happens, your son will be severely punished, but, if his defence is accepted, it will not be the extreme punishment."

When the young man had gone, Kumalo said to the English priest, "You can understand this has been a sorrowful journey. At first it was a search, and I was anxious. But as the search went on, step by step, so did the anxiety turn to fear, and this fear grew deeper step by step.

But it was here, when we heard of the murder, that my fear grew into something too great to bear." After a pause he continued. "Msimangu said to me, 'Why fear this one thing in a city where there are thousands upon thousands of people?' That comforted me, yet it did not comfort me. And even now I can hardly believe that this thing, which happens one time in a thousand, has happened to me. Sometimes, for a moment or two, I can believe that I shall wake and find it has not happened. But it is only for a moment or two. To think," said Kumalo, "that my wife and I lived out our lives in innocence, there in Ndotsheni, not knowing that this thing was coming, step by step. There is a man sleeping there in the grass, and over him is gathering the greatest storm of all his days, bringing death and destruction. People hurry home past him, to places safe from danger. And whether they do not see him there in the grass, or whether they fear to halt even a moment, they do not wake him, they let him be." They were silent a long time.

"My friend," said Father Vincent, "your anxiety turned to fear, and your fear turned to sorrow. But sorrow is better than fear. Fear is a journey, a terrible journey, but sorrow is at least an arriving."

"And where have I arrived?" asked Kumalo.

"When the storm threatens, a man is afraid for his house. But when the house is destroyed, there is something to do. About a storm he can do nothing, but he can rebuild a house."

"At my age?" asked Kumalo. "Look what has happened to the house that I built when I was young and strong. What kind of house shall I build now?"

"No one can comprehend the ways of God," said Father Vincent.

"It seems that God has turned from me," said Kumalo.

" That may seem to happen. But it does not happen, never, never, does it happen."

" I am glad to hear you," said Kumalo humbly. " But my son is now a stranger to me. I cannot touch him. I see no shame in him, no pity for those he has hurt. Tears come out of his eyes, but it seems that he weeps only for himself, he who has made two children fatherless."

" Stop," cried Father Vincent. " Go and pray, go and rest. And do not judge your son too quickly. Pray for Gertrude, and for her child, and for the girl that is to be your son's wife, and for the child that will be your grandchild. Pray for your wife and all at Ndotsheni. Pray for the soul of him who was killed, and for the woman and children that have lost him. Pray for us at the Mission House. Pray for your own rebuilding. And do not fear to pray for your son."

" I hear you," said Kumalo humbly.

" And give thanks where you can give thanks." He led the old man to the door of the Mission. " I shall pray for you," he said, " night and day. That I shall do, and anything more that you ask."

16

The next day Kumalo went alone to see the girl who was with child by his son. The girl opened the door to him, and she smiled at him uncertainly, with something that was fear, and something that was welcoming.

" Have you heard of your husband? " he asked. The smile went from her face. " I have not heard," she said.

" What I have to say is heavy," he said. " He is in prison."

"In prison?" she said.

"He is in prison, for the most terrible deed that a man can do." But the girl did not understand him. "He has killed a white man."

"Au!" The exclamation burst from her. She put her hands over her face. And Kumalo himself could not continue, for the words were like knives, cutting into a wound that was still new and open. She sat down on a box, and looked at the floor, and the tears started to run slowly down her cheeks.

"I do not wish to speak of it, my child. Can you read? The white man's newspaper?"

"A little."

"Then I shall leave it with you. I do not wish to speak of it any more. I have come to speak with you of another matter. Do you wish to marry my son?"

"It is as the umfundisi sees it."

"Is it truly your wish to marry him? I must be certain. I do not wish to take you into my family if you are unwilling."

At those words she looked up eagerly. "I am willing," she said.

"We live in a far place," he said. "There are no streets and lights there. There is only me and my wife, and the place is very quiet. You are a Zulu?"

"Yes, umfundisi."

"Where are your parents?"

"My father left my mother. They quarrelled, umfundisi. Because my mother was so often drunk."

"So your father left. And he left you also? What did you do?"

"I left that house and I lived in Sophiatown."

"Alone?"

"No, not alone."

"With your first husband?" he asked coldly. "How many have there been?"

She laughed nervously. "Only three," she said.

"And what happened to the first?"

"He was caught by the police, umfundisi."

"And the second?"

"He was caught also."

"And now the third is caught also." He stood up, and a wish to hurt her came into him. "Yes, your third is caught also, but now it is for murder. Have you had a murderer before?"

"No, no, no," she cried.

And he, seeing her, and her thin body, was ashamed for his cruelty. "How old are you, my child?"

"I do not know," she sobbed, "but I think I am sixteen."

And deep pity rose up in him. "Tell me, do you truly wish to marry my son?"

She clutched at his hands. "I wish it," she said.

"And to go to a quiet and far-off place, and be our daughter?"

"I wish it greatly," she said.

"Have you clothes for the marriage?"

"I have some clothes, umfundisi."

"And you must not live here. I shall find you a place near me. Stay well, then, my child."

"Go well, umfundisi."

He went out of the house, and she followed him to the little gate. When he turned back to look at her, she was smiling at him. He walked on like a man from whom a pain has lifted a little, not altogether, but a little. And he remembered too that Father Vincent had said, "I shall pray, night and day." At the corner he turned, and, looking back, saw that the girl was still watching him.

·   ·   ·   ·   ·   ·   ·   ·   ·

"Mrs. Lithebe, you have heard of this girl who is with child by my son. She wishes to marry my son. Then—whatever may happen—she will go with me to Ndotsheni, and bear her child there in a clean and decent home."

"You would like to bring her here, first, umfundisi?"

"Indeed, that would be a great kindness. Mother, I am grateful. Indeed, you are a mother to me."

"Why else do we live?" she said.

17

He passed again through the great gate in the grim, high wall, and they brought the boy to him. Again he took the lifeless hand in his own, and was again moved to tears, this time by the misery of his son. "Are you in health, my son?"

The son looked at one window, and then moved and looked at the other, but not at his father.

"I have some business for you, my son. Are you certain that you wish to marry this girl?"

"I can marry her."

"There is a friend of mine, a white priest, and he will see if it can be arranged. And he will get a lawyer for you."

There is a spark of life in the eyes, of some hope maybe.

"You would like a lawyer?"

"They say one can be helped by a lawyer."

"You told the police that these other two were with you?"

"I told them. And now I have told them again. And then they fetched them from their cells. And they were angry with me, and cursed me in front of the police, and said that I was trying to bring them into trouble."

"And then?"

"And then they asked what proof I had. And the only proof I had was that it was true, it was these two and no other. Then they cursed me again, and said one to the other, 'How can he lie so about us?'"

"They were your friends?"

"Yes, they were my friends."

"And they will leave you to suffer alone?"

"Now I see it."

"Be of courage, my son. Do not forget there is a lawyer. But it is only the truth you must tell him."

"I shall tell him only the truth, my father. He must come soon, my father . . . or it may be too late," he said.

"Have no fear of that. He will come soon. And Father Vincent will come to see you. And the marriage, that will be arranged. And the girl—I had not told you—she is living with me in Sophiatown. And she will come back with me to Ndotsheni, and the child will be born there."

"It is good, my father."

"And you may write now to your mother."

"I shall write, my father."

"And wipe away your tears."

The prison guard said to the boy, "You may stay here, there is a lawyer to see you. You, old man, you must go."

. . . .

Kumalo returned to the Mission House, and was having tea with Father Vincent, when the lawyer came to see them.

"I shall take the case for you, Mr. Kumalo," said the lawyer. "I shall take it *pro Deo*, as we say. It is a simple case, for the boy says simply that he fired because he was afraid, not meaning to kill. But with regard to the other two boys, I do not know what to say. I believe your son is speaking the truth. It is for me to persuade the court that your son is speaking the truth. Now I must have all the facts about your son, Mr. Kumalo, what sort of child he was, whether he was truthful and obedient, and when and why he left home, and what he has done since he came to Johannesburg. You understand?"

"I understand, sir."

"You may thank God that we have got this man," said Father Vincent, when the lawyer had gone. "He is one of the greatest lawyers in South Africa and one of the greatest friends of your people."

"I do thank God, and you too, Father. But I have one anxiety, what will it cost? My little money is nearly exhausted."

"Did you not hear him say he would take the case *pro Deo*? That is Latin, and it means, 'for God'."

"He takes it for God?"

"Yes, it will cost you nothing, or at least very little."

Kumalo stammered. "I have never met such kindness," he said. He turned away his face, for he wept easily in these days. Father Vincent smiled at him. "Go well, my friend," he said.

Book Two

BOOK TWO

I

THERE is a lovely road that runs from Ixopo into the hills.
These hills are grass-covered and rolling, and they are
lovely beyond any singing of it. The road climbs seven
miles into them, to Carisbrooke; and from there, if there is
no mist, you look down on one of the fairest valleys of
Africa. About you there is grass and you may hear the
forlorn crying of the titihoya, one of the birds of the veld.
Below you is the valley of the Umzimkulu, on its journey
from the Drakensberg Mountains to the sea; and beyond and
behind the river, great hill after great hill; and beyond and
behind them, the mountains of Ingeli and East Griqualand.

The grass is rich and thick; you cannot see the soil. It
holds the rain and the mist, and they sink slowly into the
ground, feeding the streams in every small valley. It is
well looked after, and not too many cattle feed upon it; not
too many fires burn it, laying bare the soil.

Up here on the tops is a small and lovely valley, between
two hills that shelter it. There is a house there, and flat
ploughed fields; they will tell you that it is one of the finest
farms of this countryside. It is called High Place, the farm
and dwelling-place of James Jarvis, Esquire, and it stands
high above Ndotsheni, and the great valley of the Umzimkulu.

.   .   .   .

Jarvis watched the ploughing with a gloomy eye. The hot afternoon sun of October poured down on the fields, and there was no cloud in the sky. Rain, rain, there was no rain. The lumps of earth turned up hard and unbroken, and here and there the plough would ride uselessly over the iron soil.

Jarvis, calling his dog, set out along the path that led to the tops. Up there was grass, fed by the mists, but below the tops the grass was dry, and the hills of Ndotsheni were red and bare. Something might have been done if these people had only learned how to build walls to save the soil from washing away in the rains, and if they had ploughed along the contours of the hills. But the hills were steep, and the oxen were weak, so that it was easier to plough downwards. And the people were ignorant, and knew nothing about farming methods.

Some people said there must be more education, but a boy with education did not want to work on the farms, and went off to the towns to look for an easier occupation with more money. The work was done by old men and women, and when the grown men came back from the mines and the towns, they sat in the sun and drank their liquor and made endless conversation.

Jarvis turned these old thoughts over in his mind as he sat on the hill-top. Down in the valley below there was a car going up to his house. He recognized it as the police-car from Ixopo, and it would probably be the police captain making his usual daily tour of the district. His wife was coming out of the house to meet the car, and there were two policemen climbing out of it. His wife was pointing up to the tops. He called his dog, and set out along the path, and about half-way down to the fields, he met the two police officers.

" Well, captain, have you brought some rain for us? "

"No, Mr. Jarvis. I am sorry, but I have bad news for you."

"Bad news? Is it my son?" he asked.

"Yes, Mr. Jarvis."

"Is he dead?"

"Yes, Mr. Jarvis." The captain paused. "He was shot dead this afternoon in Johannesburg."

"Shot dead? By whom?"

"It is suspected by a native housebreaker."

"My God!" he said, and then, "You didn't tell my wife?"

"No, Mr. Jarvis."

"She isn't strong. I don't know how she will stand it."

"Mr. Jarvis, I am instructed to offer you every assistance. You could take an aeroplane and be in Johannesburg at midnight."

"Yes, yes. We'll take it."

In a few minutes they were at the house.

"James, what's the matter?"

"Some trouble, my dear. Come with me to the office,"

The captain went to the telephone. He began to talk to Police Headquarters about the aeroplane. And he put his hand over his open ear to shut out the sound of the woman, of her crying and sobbing.

2

A young man met them at the airport.

"Mr. and Mrs. Jarvis?"

"Yes."

"I'm John Harrison, Mary's brother." Mary was their dead son's wife. "I don't think you remember me. I was only a youngster when you saw me last. Let me carry your things. I've a car here for you. Mary and the children are at my mother's, and we're expecting you both to stay with us."

In the car he said to them, " Mr. Jarvis, Arthur was the finest man I ever knew."

" How is Mary? "

" She's suffering from the shock, Mr. Jarvis, but she's very brave."

" And the children? "

" They've taken it very badly, Mr. Jarvis. And that has given Mary something to occupy herself."

Late that evening, as the men sat talking, Mary's father told Jarvis of the essay his son Arthur had been writing just before he was killed, on " The Truth About Native Crime."

" My son and I didn't see eye to eye on the native question," said Jarvis, " but I'd like to see what he wrote."

" My father and I don't see eye to eye on the native question either, Mr. Jarvis," said the younger Harrison. " You know there was no one in South Africa who thought so deeply about it, and no one who thought so clearly, as Arthur did. 'And what else is there to think deeply and clearly about in South Africa?' he used to say."

Harrison told Jarvis how the messages had poured into the house. " Messages from every kind of person," he said. " From the Bishop and from white politicians, and from coloured people, and Indians, and Jews. There was talk of getting him to stand at the next election as a representative for the natives."

" I didn't know that."

" Yes, he was always speaking here and there. Native crime, and more native schools, and hospitals."

Jarvis filled his pipe slowly, and listened to this tale of his son, to this tale of a stranger.

" I warned him once," said Harrison, "that he would lose his business with the Europeans, and told him there was Mary to consider. 'I've spoken to Mary,' he said to me. 'She and I agree that it's more important to speak the truth than to make money.'"

Jarvis did not speak. For this boy of his had gone journeying in strange waters, further than his parents had known. Or perhaps his mother knew. It would not surprise him if his mother knew. Soon afterwards they said good night, and Jarvis went up to bed and told his wife all that Harrison had told him.

" It makes me proud," she whispered.

" But you always knew he was like that? "

" Yes, I knew. It's easier for a mother, James."

" I suppose so. It was a good life he led. I'm sorry I didn't understand it." Then he said in a whisper, " I didn't know it would ever be so important to understand it. There's one thing I don't understand, why it should have happened to him."

3

Jarvis sat in the chair of his son, in his son's study. On the table were papers in his son's handwriting. They were obviously part of some larger whole, for the first line was the end of a sentence, and the last line was a sentence unfinished.

" . . . was permissible. What we did when we came to South Africa was permissible. It was permissible to develop our great resources with the aid of what labour we could find. It was permissible to use unskilled men for unskilled work. But it is not permissible to keep men unskilled for the sake of unskilled work.

" It was permissible when we discovered gold to bring labour to the mines. It was permissible to build compounds and to keep women and children away from the towns. But in the light of what we know now, it is no longer permissible. It is not permissible for us to go on destroying family life when we know that we are destroying it.

" It is not permissible to develop any resources if they can be developed only by a policy of keeping labour poor. It is not permissible to add to one's possessions if this can only be done at the cost of other men.

" It was permissible to leave native education to those who wanted to develop it. It was permissible to doubt its benefits. But it is no longer permissible in the light of what we know. There is now a large native population in the towns. Society must educate its children so that they grow up to obey the society's laws, and realize the aims and purposes of the society. There is no other way that it can be done.

" It was permissible to allow the destruction of a tribal system that prevented the growth of the country. But it is not permissible to watch its destruction, and to replace it by nothing, so that a whole people goes rotten, physically and morally.

" The old tribal system was, for all its violence and superstition, a moral system. Our natives to-day produce criminals, not because it is their nature to do so, but because their simple system of order and tradition has been destroyed. It was destroyed by our own civilization. Our civilization has therefore an unavoidable duty to set up another system of order and tradition. It is time . . ."

And there the manuscript and the page ended. Jarvis searched amongst the papers on the table, but he could find nothing more. He sat smoking his pipe and was lost in thought.

Unasked, unwanted, the picture of the small boy came to his mind, the small boy at High Place.

4

The funeral was over. "You're welcome to stay here, Jarvis," said Harrison, "as long as you are wanted in Johannesburg. What did the police say, if I may ask?"

"They're still waiting for the servant-boy to recover. They have hopes that he recognized one of them. They hope too that someone may have seen them getting away."

"I hope to God they get them. And string them all up. Pardon me, Jarvis."

"I know exactly what you mean."

"We're not safe, Jarvis. I don't even know that stringing them up will make us safe. Sometimes I think the problem has got beyond us."

"I know what you mean. But myself—perhaps it's too soon to think about it."

"I know what *you* mean. I understand—that side of it isn't the side you feel about the most."

"You're right, it's not that side of it that seems important, not yet anyway. But I realize there *is* another side to it."

"We've been demanding more police. I'm not a native-hater, Jarvis; I try to give them decent wages, and a clean room, and reasonable time off. Our servants stay with us for years. But the natives as a whole are getting out of control. They've even started Trade Unions. They're threatening to strike here in the mines for ten shillings a day. They get about three shillings now, and some of the mines are near closing down. They live in decent compounds—some of the latest compounds I wouldn't mind living in myself. They get good food, far better than they ever get at home, free medical attention, and God knows what. I tell you, Jarvis, if mining costs go up much more there won't be any mines. And where will South Africa be then? And where would the natives be themselves? They'd die by the thousands of starvation. I tell you there wouldn't be any South Africa at all if it weren't for the mines."

There was silence for a time, and then Jarvis said, "Harrison, I'm going to bed. It's done me good to listen to you. I haven't done much talking myself; it's not because I'm not interested. I'm sure you understand. But I could have wished that he was here to-night, that I could have heard him argue with you."

"I didn't agree with him," said Harrison, "but I had a great respect for anything that he said."

The next morning Harrison called Jarvis early. "The police have just telephoned, Jarvis. The boy recovered consciousness this morning. He says there were three right enough, and he is sure that the one that knocked him out was an old garden boy of your son's. The police are after him now. They certainly seem to be moving."

5

At the head of the Court is a high seat where the Judge sits. The Judge does not make the Law. It is the People that make the Law. It is the duty of a Judge to do justice, but it is only the People than can be just.

In South Africa men are proud of their Judges, because they are incorruptible. Even the black men have faith in them, though they do not always have faith in the Law. In a land of fear this incorruptibility is like a lamp set upon a stand, giving light to all that are in the house.

. . . .

They call for silence in the Court, and the people stand. And the Judge enters. The Court is begun.

The three that are to be judged come in. Absalom Kumalo, Matthew Kumalo and Johannes Pafuri. The lawyer for the Government speaks for a long time, and tells the Court the whole story of the crime. And Absalom Kumalo is still and silent, but the other two look grieved and shocked to think such things are said.

" Why did you carry this revolver? " asks the lawyer.

" It was to frighten the servant of the house," says Absalom.

" If this revolver is to frighten people, why must it be loaded? "

But the boy does not answer. . . . Questions, questions, questions. And later, " I was afraid, I was afraid. I never meant to shoot him." And then more questions.

6

There is little attention being paid to the trial of those accused of the murder of Arthur Jarvis of Parkwold. For gold has been discovered, more gold, rich gold, in a little place called Odendaalsrust. Yesterday it was quite unknown, to-day it is one of the famous places of the world.

The gold is as rich as any gold that has ever been discovered in South Africa, as rich as anything in Johannesburg. Men are saying that a new Johannesburg will rise there, a great city of tall buildings and busy streets. Men that were gloomy because the gold in Johannesburg could not last for ever, are happy and excited. There is excitement in Johannesburg. Men go mad, for the shares are climbing in price to heights that are beyond expectation.

Gold, gold, gold. The country is going to be rich again. Shares are up from twenty shillings to a hundred shillings; think of it; thank God for it. There are people, it is true, who are not very thankful. But it must be admitted that they hold no shares at all. Some of these people are saying it would be nice if these shares could have stayed at twenty shillings, and the other eighty shillings have been used to save the soil of the country, to build boys' clubs and girls' clubs, and to have more hospitals, and pay more to the miners.

Well, say those who have the shares, anyone can see that this thinking is muddled, because the price of shares has really nothing to do with the question of wages at all. And perhaps a great city will grow up at Odendaalsrust, a second Johannesburg.

.   .   .   .

But money is not something to go mad about. And no second Johannesburg is needed upon the earth. One is enough.

7

Jarvis had just reached the last paragraphs of another of his son's essays which the younger Harrison had brought for him to read.

"Therefore I shall devote myself, my time, my energy, my talents, to the service of South Africa. I shall no longer ask myself if this or that is advantageous, but only if it is right. I shall do this, not because I am noble or unselfish, but because life slips away, and because I need for the rest of my journey a star that will not play false to me. . . ."

There was a knock at the kitchen door, and he went out to find a native priest standing there. The priest was old, and his black clothes were green with age, and his collar was brown with age. He took off his hat, showing the whiteness of his head, and he looked afraid and he was trembling.

"Good morning, umfundisi," said Jarvis in Zulu. The priest answered in a trembling voice, "Sir," and to Jarvis's surprise, he sat down on the lowest step, as though he were ill or starving.

"Are you ill, umfundisi? Do you wish water? Or is it food? Are you hungry?"

"No, sir, I shall recover." Slowly the old priest stood up. "You are from Ndotsheni, sir?" he said.

"Yes, I come from Ndotsheni. But you are in fear of me, and I do not know what it is."

"It is true, sir. It is very heavy. It is the heaviest thing of all my years."

"Tell me," said Jarvis. "It will lighten you."

"Then," said the old man, "this thing that is the heaviest thing of all my years, is the heaviest thing of all your years also."

Jarvis looked at him. "You can mean only one thing," he said, "you can mean only one thing."

"It was my son that killed your son," said the old man. So they were silent.

"I have heard you. I understand what I did not understand. There is no anger in me."

"I have seen you riding past Ndotsheni, sir, past the church where I work."

"Perhaps you saw the boy also," said Jarvis. "He too used to ride past Ndotsheni. On a red horse with a white face. And he carried wooden guns, here in his belt, as small boys do."

"I remember, sir. There was a brightness in him."

"Yes, yes," said Jarvis, "there was a brightness in him."

Again they were silent. The old man started to walk down the path to the back gate. As he turned to close it he saw that Jarvis had followed him, and he bowed to him.

"Go well, umfundisi," said Jarvis.

"Stay well, sir."

As Jarvis returned to the house his wife came to meet him. "Why are you so disturbed, James?" she asked.

"Something that came out of the past," he said. "You know how it comes, suddenly?"

She was satisfied, and said, "I know." She held his arm more closely.

8

The great bull voice is speaking there in the square. There are many policemen there, both white and black, to keep order, because there are those who can be moved by the sound of the voice alone. For the voice has magic in it, and it has threatening in it, and it is as though Africa itself were in it. A lion growls in it, and thunder echoes in it over the black mountains.

"We do not ask for what cannot be given," says John Kumalo. "We ask only for our share of what is produced by our labour. New gold has been found, and South Africa is rich again. This gold will stay in the depths of the earth if we do not dig it out. I do not say it is our gold, I say only that we should get our share in it. It is the gold of the whole people, the white and the black, and the coloured. But who will get the most of this gold?" And here the voice growls in the bull throat. A wave of excitement passes through the crowd. The policemen stand more alert, except those who have heard this before. For they know that this Kumalo goes so far and no further. What if this voice should say words that it speaks already in private, should rise and not fall again, should rise and rise and rise, and the people rise with it, should madden them with thoughts of rebellion and with thoughts of power and possession? It would not be hard to do, it does not need a brain to think such words. But the man is afraid, and the deep thundering growl dies down, and the people shiver and come to themselves.

But when the voice growls again, the crowd stirs as though a great wind were blowing through it. Here is the moment, John Kumalo, for the great voice to reach even to the gates of Heaven. But he knows the great power that he has, the power of which he is afraid. And the voice dies away, as thunder dies away over mountains, and echoes and re-echoes more and more faintly.

There are those who know that to go to prison would bring greatness to them, there are those who would go to prison not caring if it brought greatness or not. But John Kumalo is not one of them. There is no applause in prison.

.   .   .   .

The times are anxious, there can be no doubt about that. The strike has come and gone. It never went beyond the mines. The worst trouble was at a place where the police were called in to drive the black miners into the mine. There was fighting, and three of the black miners were killed. But all is quiet, they report, all is quiet.

.   .   .   .

In the deserted harbour there is water that moves endlessly against the stone walls. In the dark and silent forest there is a leaf that falls. Behind the polished panelling the white ant eats away the wood. Nothing is ever quiet, except for fools.

9

Mrs. Lithebe called Gertrude into the house. "I have done my best to understand you, my daughter. But I do not succeed in it."

"I did no wrong."

"I did not say you did wrong. But you do not understand this house, you do not understand the people that live in it."

Gertrude stood sullenly. "I do understand it," she said.

"Then why do you speak with such people, my daughter?"

"I did not know they were not decent people."

"Do you not hear the way they speak, the way they laugh? Do you not hear them laugh idly and carelessly?"

"I did not know it was wrong."

"I did not say it was wrong. It is idle and careless, the way they speak and laugh. Are you not trying to be a good woman? Then such people will not help you. Your brother the umfundisi has surely suffered enough."

"He has suffered."

"Then do not make him suffer further, my daughter."

"I shall be glad to leave this place," Gertrude said. "I do not know what to do in this place."

"It is not this place only," said Mrs. Lithebe. "Even in Ndotsheni you will find those who are ready to laugh and speak carelessly."

"It is this place," said Gertrude. "I have known nothing but trouble in this Johannesburg. I shall be glad to be gone."

"It will not be long before you go, for the case will finish to-morrow."

There was a knock at the door, and a woman neighbour came in. "There is a bad thing in the newspaper," she said, and she showed the other women the headlines.

ANOTHER MURDER TRAGEDY IN CITY.
EUROPEAN SHOT DEAD BY NATIVE HOUSEBREAKER.

They were shocked. "It is a hard thing that this should happen at this moment," said the woman, "just when the case is to finish."

Mrs. Lithebe heard the click of the gate, and threw the paper under a chair. It was Kumalo and the girl. The girl was holding his arm, for he was frail in these days. She guided him to his room, and they were hardly gone before Msimangu entered. His eyes fell on the paper at once. "Has he seen it?" he asked.

"No, umfundisi. Is it not a hard thing that this should happen at this moment?"

"This judge is a great judge," said Msimangu. "But it is a hard thing as you say. He likes to read the paper. What shall we do?"

"There is no other paper here," said Mrs. Lithebe. "But when he goes to eat at the Mission House he will see it."

"That is why I came," said Msimangu. "Mother, could we not eat here to-night?"

"That is a small thing to ask. There is food enough, though it is simple."

"Indeed, mother, you are always our helper."

"For what else are we born?" she said.

So they hid the newspaper, and they all ate at Mrs. Lithebe's.

10

The people stand when the great Judge comes into the Court, they stand more solemnly to-day, for this is the day of the judgment. The Judge sits, and then the people; and then the three accused are brought from the place under the Court.

"I have given long thought and consideration to this case," says the Judge. "I have listened carefully to all the evidence that has been brought forward, and have tested it piece by piece."

Very carefully, and in great detail, the Judge goes through the evidence as to whether it was Matthew Kumalo and Johannes Pafuri who were with Absalom Kumalo when he shot Arthur Jarvis.

And at last, "I have come to the conclusion that the guilt of the second and third accused is not established, and they will be accordingly discharged."

The accused Absalom Kumalo makes no sign. He does not even look at the two who are now free. But Pafuri looks about as though he would say: "This is right, this is just."

"There remains the case against the first accused," says the Judge, "and he admits freely that he shot Arthur Jarvis. His lawyer draws attention to his youth and to the disastrous effect of a great and wicked city on the character of a simple tribal boy. He has told us of the disaster that has overwhelmed our native tribal society, and of the responsibility of white society for this disaster. But even if this is true, there is nevertheless a Law, and the judges must administer the Law. A Judge may not fail to administer the Law because the society is imperfect. If the Law is the law of a society that some feel to be unjust, it is the Law and the society that must be changed."

Again the careful and detailed review of the evidence—this time about Absalom Kumalo. . . . "This young man goes to a house with the intention to break in and steal. He takes with him a loaded revolver. He says that it was not his intention to kill. Why then must it be loaded? . . . He says he had no intention to kill, and that he fired the revolver out of fear. But it is true that he took with him a weapon the use of which might well result in the death of any man who interfered with the carrying out of his stealing. The Law on this point . . ." and so on, until the end.

.   .   .   .

They are silent in the Court. The Judge speaks:

"This Court finds you guilty, Absalom Kumalo, of the murder of Arthur Trevelyan Jarvis. Have you anything to say before I sentence you?"

"I have only this to say, that I killed this man, but I did not mean to kill him, only I was afraid."

They are silent in the Court.

"I sentence you, Absalom Kumalo, to be hanged by the neck until you are dead. And may the Lord have mercy upon your soul."

.   .   .   .

The Judge rises, and the people rise. But not all is silent. The guilty one falls to the floor, crying and sobbing. And there is a woman wailing, and an old man crying, "Oh God, oh, my God." No one calls for silence, though the

Judge is not quite gone. For who can stop the heart from breaking?

They come out of the Court, the white on one side, the black on the other, according to the custom. But Father Vincent and the young white man break the custom, and they and Msimangu help the old and broken man. It is not often that such a custom is broken. It is only when there is a deep experience that such a custom is broken.

11

They passed again through the great gate in the grim, high wall, Father Vincent and Kumalo and Gertrude and the girl Absalom was to marry and Msimangu.

The boy and girl greeted each other like strangers, each giving hands without life, to be held loosely, so that the hands fell apart easily. And Kumalo said desperately to his son, " Are you in health? " And the boy answered, " I am greatly. Are you in health, my father? " So Kumalo said, " I am greatly." He longed for other things to say, but he could not find them.

Then Father Vincent married Absalom and the girl. After it was done, the priest and the wife and Gertrude left father and son, and Kumalo said to him, " I am glad you are married."

" I am also glad, my father."

" I shall care for your child, my son."

" And you will tell my mother that I remember her? "

" Yes, indeed, I shall tell her."

" When does my father return to Ndotsheni? "

" To-morrow, my son."

" To-morrow? "

" Yes, to-morrow."

At these words the boy fell on the floor, and began to sob. For a boy is afraid of death. The old man knelt by his son. "Be of courage, my son."

"I am afraid," he cried, "I am afraid."

The prison guard came in and said, "Old man, you must go now."

"My son, I must go now." He stood up, but the boy caught his father by the knees, and cried out to him, "You must not leave me, you must not leave me." He broke out again into the terrible sobbing. The prison guard said again, "Old man, you must go now." And Kumalo said to Absalom, "Stay well, my son," but the boy did not hear him.

And so they parted.

Heavy with grief, Kumalo left him, and went out to the gate in the wall where the others were waiting. And the girl came to him, and said shyly, but with a smile, "Umfundisi."

"Yes, my child."

"I am now your daughter."

"It is true," he said.

.   .   .   .

Kumalo went to see his brother. "I am come to say farewell to you, my brother."

"Well, well, you are returning to Ndotsheni. You have been a long time away, my brother, and your wife will be glad to see you. When are you leaving?"

"We leave to-morrow at nine o'clock."

"So Gertrude is going with you. And her child. You are doing a good thing, my brother. Johannesburg is not a place for a woman alone."

"I am taking another child also," said Kumalo. "The wife of my son. And she too is with child."

"Well, well, I have heard of it," said John Kumalo. "That is another good thing you are doing."

"My brother, there is a matter that must be spoken between us."

"It is as you wish, my brother."

"I have not come here to reproach you——"

"Reproach me? Why should you reproach me? There was a case and a judge. That is not for you or me or any other person."

"I do not say that I should reproach you. As you say, there is a case and a judge. There is also a Great Judge, but of Him you and I do not speak. But there is quite another matter."

"Well, well. What is this matter?"

"One thing is to greet you before I go. But I could not greet you and say nothing. You have seen how it is with my son. He left his home and he was eaten up. What of your own son? He also has left his home."

"I am thinking about this matter," said John Kumalo. "When this trouble is finished, I shall bring him back here." He laughed his bull laugh. "I cannot leave all the good deeds to you, my brother."

"And there is one last thing," said Kumalo.

"You are my older brother. Speak what you wish."

"Your politics, my brother. Where are they taking you?"

"My politics, my brother, are my own. I do not speak to you about your religion."

"You said: 'Speak what you wish.'"

"Well, well, I did say it. But I know what I am fighting for. You have read history. History teaches that the men who do the work cannot be kept down for ever. If they will stand together, who will stand against them?"

" You mean if they strike? "

" Yes, I mean that."

" But the last strike was not successful."

John Kumalo stood on his feet, and his voice growled in his throat. " Look what they did to us," he said. " They forced us into the mines as though we were slaves. Have we no right to keep back our labour? "

" Do you hate the white man, my brother? "

John Kumalo looked at him with suspicion. " I hate no man," he said. " I hate only injustice."

" I have heard that you have said dangerous things, here in this shop. I have heard that they are watching you. I say this because you are my brother."

Have no doubt it is fear in the eyes. The big man looks like a boy that is caught. " In this shop? Who would know what is said in this shop? "

For all his wish to forgive, Kumalo's desire to hurt was stronger, so strong that he was tempted to lie; yielded, and lied. " I have heard," he said, " that a man might have been sent to this shop to deceive you. As a friend."

The big bull man wiped the sweat of fear from his brow. " You heard that? "

And Kumalo, ashamed, had to say, " I heard it."

" What a friend! " said the bull man. " What a friend! "

And Kumalo cried at him out of his suffering, " My son had two such friends."

The big man looked at him, and understood. " Out of my shop," he roared, " out of my shop." He kicked over the table and came at Kumalo, so that the old man had to step out of the door into the street, and the door was shut against him. Out there in the street, he was ashamed. He had come to tell his brother that power corrupts, that a man who fights for justice must himself be clean, that love is greater than force. And none of these things had he done.

"God have mercy on me," he said. He turned to the door, but it was locked. Brother had shut out brother.

The people were watching, so he walked away in his distress.

.   .   .   .

Msimangu gave a party at Mrs. Lithebe's that evening. It was not a gay party, but the food was plentiful, and there was some sad pleasure in it. Msimangu made a speech about his brother priest, Kumalo, and Mrs. Lithebe's kindness to them all. Kumalo made a speech too, but it was weak and uncertain, for the lie and the quarrel were in his mind. But he thanked Msimangu and Mrs. Lithebe for all their kindnesses.

Then Msimangu told them that he had news for them. He was retiring into a religious community, and would give up the world and all possessions. They finished with prayers, and afterwards Msimangu said to Kumalo. "I am giving up all possessions, but I have saved a little money. And I have permission from the Church to give this to you, to help you with all the money you have spent in Johannesburg, and all your new duties." He put a Post Office Book into Kumalo's hand.

Kumalo said, "In all my days I have known no one as you are."

And Msimangu said sharply: "I am only a weak man, and I ask that you will pray for me in this new thing I am about to do."

"I shall pray for you, morning and evening, all my days."

"Good night, brother."

"Good night, Msimangu, friend of friends. And may God watch over you always."

"And you also."

Kumalo watched him go down the street.

In the morning he rose early. He opened the door quietly, and shook the girl gently. "It is time for us to go," he said.

"I shall not be long," she said.

He smiled at the eagerness. "Ndotsheni," he said, "to-morrow it is Ndotsheni." He opened Gertrude's door. But Gertrude was gone. The little boy was there, the red dress he had bought her was there. But Gertrude was gone.

Book Three

BOOK THREE

I

THE engine steams and whistles over the veld. The white, flat hills of the mines drop behind, and the country rolls away as far as the eye can see. They sit all together, Kumalo, and the little boy on his knee, and the girl. The little boy has asked for his mother, but Kumalo tells him that she has gone away, and he does not ask any more.

Darkness falls, and they thunder through the night. As the sun rises they wind down the greatest hills of all, to Pietermaritzburg, the lovely city. Here they enter another train, and the train runs along the valley where the tribes live, and the soil is sick. And the people tell Kumalo that the rains will not fall; they cannot plough or plant, and there will be hunger in this valley.

They enter the last train, that runs beside the lovely road that goes into the hills. Many people know him, and he is afraid of their questions. They talk like children, these people, and it is nothing to ask: "Who is this person? Who is this girl? Who is this child? Where do they come from? Where do they go?" They will ask: "How is your sister? How is your son?", so he takes his sacred book and reads it to prevent their questions.

The sun is setting over the great valley of the Umzimkulu, behind the mountains. His wife is there, and a friend to help the umfundisi with his bags. He goes to his wife quickly. She looks her question, and he says to her, "Our son is to die; perhaps there may be mercy, but let us not talk of it now."

"I understand you," she says.

"And Gertrude. All was ready for her to come. But when I went to wake her, she was gone. And this is the small boy, and this is our new daughter." Kumalo's wife lifts the small boy and kisses him. "You are my child," she says. She puts him down and takes the girl in her arms, and says to her, "You are my daughter."

Kumalo shakes hands with his friend, and they all set out on the narrow path that leads into the valley of Ndotsheni. Here a man calls, "Umfundisi, you are back, it is a good thing." And here a woman says to another, "Look, it is the umfundisi that has returned." A child comes into the path. "We are glad that the umfundisi is here again," she says.

The path is dropping into the red land of Ndotsheni. It is a wasted land, a land of old men and women and children, but it is home. The maize hardly grows to the height of a man, but it is home.

"It is dry here, umfundisi. We cry for rain."

"I have heard it, my friend."

"Our maize is nearly finished, umfundisi. It is known to God alone what we shall eat. And the stream has been dry for a month, umfundisi."

"Where do we get water, then?"

"The women must go to the river, umfundisi, that comes from the place of Jarvis."

At the name of Jarvis, Kumalo feels fear and pain, but he makes himself say, "How is Mr. Jarvis?"

"He returned yesterday, umfundisi. I do not know how he is. But his wife returned some weeks ago, and she is sick and thin."

They do not speak again, and the path runs past the huts. In the dusk one voice calls to another in some far-distant place. If you are a Zulu you can hear what they say, but if you are not, even if you know the language, you would find it hard to know what is being called. Some white men call it magic, but it is no magic. It is Africa, the beloved country.

"They call that you are returned, umfundisi."

"I hear it, my friend."

"They are satisfied."

The call comes from the huts and the hills—"Umfundisi, you have returned."

There is a lamp outside the church, and as Kumalo and his wife approach, the men and women there lift their voices into a hymn of thanks to God for His mercy.

And Kumalo must pray. He prays aloud with the people. "God, we give thanks. . . . God, give us rain. . . ." And at last, "And God, my son . . . forgive him his wickedness."

It is done, it is out, the hard thing that was so feared.

"The Lord bless you and keep you, and give you peace, now and for ever. And the love of God be with you, now and for ever."

They rise, and they sing a new song, "God save Africa."

Yes, God save Africa, the beloved country. God save us from fear. God save us all.

.   .   .   .

The people have all gone now, and Kumalo turns to his friend. "There are things that I must tell you. My sister Gertrude was to come with us. But when I went to wake her, she was gone. And my son, he is to be hanged. You may tell your friends. It is not a thing that can be hidden. I do not know if I should stay here."

" Why, umfundisi? "

" What, with a sister who has left her child, and a son who has killed a man? Who am I to stay here? "

" Umfundisi, it must be what you desire. But I tell you that there is not one man or woman that would desire it. There is not one man or woman here that has not grieved for you, that is not satisfied that you are returned. Why, could you not see? "

" I have seen and it has touched me. It is something, after all that has been suffered. I have lived so long here, I could not desire to leave it. And I have learned a secret. Pain and suffering, they are a secret. Kindness and love, they are a secret. But I have learned that kindness and love pay for pain and suffering."

Kumalo walked to his little house. When the girl had gone to bed, Kumalo gave Msimangu's Post Office Book to his wife.

She opened it and cried out when she saw that there was thirty pounds in it. " Is it ours? " she asked.

" It is ours," he said. " It is a gift, from the best man of all my days. Sit down, and I shall tell you about Msimangu, and about other matters."

She sat down, trembling. " I am listening," she said.

2

Kumalo began to pray regularly in his church for the restoration of Ndotsheni. But he knew that was not enough. Men must come together and do something. He went to see the chief and asked him to help. But the chief was old and had no useful word to say. So Kumalo went out again into the heat to seek the headmaster of the school. But the headmaster shook his head, and talked about

economic causes, and said that the school was a place of
little power. Sad and tired, Kumalo walked back again to
his house. Suddenly he caught his breath in astonishment,
for there was a small white boy on a red horse, a small
white boy as like to another who had ridden here as any
could be. The boy smiled at Kumalo, and said, "Good
morning."

"Good morning," said Kumalo. "It is a hot day for
riding." The boy got off his horse, and they talked as an
old man and a young child do talk, with many questions.
And the boy proudly used some Zulu words. "That is
right," said Kumalo. "Would you like a drink of water?
You are hot."

"I would like a drink of milk," said the boy.

"There is no milk in Ndotsheni."

The small boy said quietly, "I would like water, umfundisi."

Kumalo brought him the water and asked him, "How
long are you staying here?"

"Not very long now, umfundisi. These are not our real
holidays now. We are here for special reasons."

And Kumalo said in his heart, "O fatherless child, I know
your reasons."

"Why is there no milk in Ndotsheni?" asked the boy.
"What do the children do?"

Kumalo looked at him. "They die, my child."

"Doesn't the doctor come?"

"Yes, and he says the children must have milk."

And the small boy said in a small voice, "I see." He
walked to his horse. "Good-bye, umfundisi."

.   .   .   .

The night brought coolness. While they were having
their meal the friend who had carried the bags came. "I

have a message for you from Mr. Jarvis." Kumalo had a dull sense of fear. "And come and look what I have brought you." There outside the door was milk, in shining cans in a cart. "The milk is for small children. And it is to be given by you only. And each morning I shall take back the cans, and in the evening I shall bring them back full. This will be done till the grass comes and we have milk again. Where shall I put the cans, umfundisi?"

But Kumalo was dumb and stupid. And the man said, "God will bless him," and Kumalo nodded.

3

Letters came from Johannesburg. There was to be no mercy for Absalom. He was to be hanged on the fifteenth day of that month.

Kumalo and his wife read this news and could say nothing to each other. At last Kumalo lifted his eyes and looked out of the windows. "Look," he said, "look at the clouds." She came and stood by him, and saw the great heavy clouds that were gathering on the other side of the Umzimkulu valley. "It will rain," he said.

He went out to look at the clouds, then stood there reading Msimangu's letter. He remained motionless as he read the last lines again. "Father Vincent tells me that Mr. Jarvis has given one thousand pounds to the African Boys' Club of which his son was President."

While he stood there he saw a motor-car coming down the road into the valley. Then he saw that not far from the church there was a white man sitting still upon a horse, waiting for the car. It was Jarvis. For an hour, Jarvis and the men from the car measured distances on the ground and planted sticks in the ground, as if they were surveying it for some building or other. They had scarcely finished when the storm broke. The men hurried off in the car, but Jarvis saw Kumalo, who had gone to the church, and called, "Umfundisi, may I stay in your church?"

So they went into the church. But it was not long before the rain found holes in the old rusted roof, and Jarvis had to move to avoid it. It was not until the storm was nearly over that Jarvis, without looking at the old man, said, "Is there mercy?" Kumalo took the letter from his pocket with trembling hands, and Jarvis read it. "I understand," he said. "When it comes to the fifteenth day, I shall remember. Stay well, umfundisi."

He mounted his horse and rode away.

4

The sticks stood where the men had put them, and it was rumoured that a dam was to be built here. It would be filled by a great pipe bringing water from the river at High Place. Kumalo's friend told him that Jarvis had gone away to Pretoria, and his business was the business of the dam.

One day a young man came to Kumalo's house. "You are the umfundisi? I am the new agricultural demonstrator."

"Come into the house," said Kumalo, excited. "Who sent you to me?"

"Why, the white man who brought me, Mr. Jarvis. He is paying me to work here. I come to Ndotsheni to teach farming, umfundisi."

So the young man told the people how they must stop ploughing up and down the hills, how they must plant trees. Some must give up their ground for trees, and some for pastures. But these were hard things to do, because the people must learn that it is harmful for each man to try to earn a living from his own little piece of ground. But the young man was hopeful.

"Umfundisi," said the young man, "there is no reason why this valley should not be what it was before. But it will not happen quickly. Not in a day."

"If God wills," said Kumalo humbly, "before I die. For I have lived my life in destruction."

5

Over the great valley the storm-clouds were gathering again in the heavy heat. Kumalo looked at the sky, and then was surprised to see his friend driving along the road, with the cart that brought the milk. "You are early, my friend."

"I am early, umfundisi," said his friend gravely. "We work no more to-day. The wife of Mr. Jarvis is dead."

"Au! Au! It is a sorrow. And Mr. Jarvis?"

"He goes about silent. You know what sort of man he is."

Kumalo went into the house, and with great difficulty wrote a letter.

SIR,

We are grieved here at this church to hear that the mother has passed away. We are certain that she knew of the things you have done for us, and did something in it. We shall pray in this church for the rest of her soul, and for you also in your suffering.

Your faithful servant,
(REV.) S. KUMALO.

And later came an answer.

UMFUNDISI,

   I thank you for your message of sympathy, and for the promise of the prayers of your church. You are right, my wife knew of the things that are being done, and had the greatest part in it. These things we did in memory of our beloved son. It was one of her last wishes that a new church should be built at Ndotsheni, and I shall come to discuss it with you.

 You should know that my wife was suffering before we went to Johannesburg.

Yours truly,

JAMES JARVIS.

6

There is ploughing in Ndotsheni, and indeed on all the farms around it. But the ploughing goes slowly, because the young demonstrator tells the men they must no longer go up and down. They must throw up walls of earth, and plough round the hills, so that the fields look no longer like they used to look in the old days of ploughing.

There has been much silence, and much sullenness. No one was more dissatisfied than those who had to give up their fields. And yet there is something new in this valley, some spirit and some life, and much to talk about in the huts. Although nothing has come yet, something is here already.

  .   .   .   .

"You can be proud," said Kumalo to the young demonstrator. "For there is a new life in this valley. I have been here for many years, but I have never seen ploughing with such spirit. It is not only these rains. There is hope here, such as I have never seen before."

"You must not expect too much," said the young man anxiously. "I do not expect much this year. The maize will be a little higher, and the harvest a little bigger, but the soil is poor indeed."

"How long will it be before the trees are ready?"

"Many years. Tell me, umfundisi, do you think the people will bear the winter for seven years?"

"Have courage, young man. Both the chief and I are working for you."

"I am impatient for the dam," said the demonstrator. "When the dam is made, there will be water for the pastures. There will be milk in this valley. It will not be necessary to take the white man's milk."

Kumalo looked at him. "Where would we be without the white man's milk?" he asked. "Where would we be without all that this white man has done for us? Where would you be also? Would you be working for him here?"

"It is true I am paid by him. I am not ungrateful."

"Then you should not speak so," said Kumalo coldly.

"I understand you," said the young man. "This man is a good man, and I respect him. Umfundisi, I work here with all my heart because I work for my country and my people. I could not work so for any master. It was the white man who gave us so little land, it was the white man who took us away from the land to go to work. And if this valley were restored, as you are always asking in your prayers, do you think it would hold all the people of the tribe if they returned?"

"I do not know, indeed."

"But I know, umfundisi. We can restore this valley for those who are here, but when the children grow up, there will again be too many. Some will have to go still."

And Kumalo was silent, having no answer.

"We work for Africa," said the young man, "not for this man or that man. Not for a white man or a black man, but for Africa."

The young man went into the house, and Kumalo stood for a moment in the dark, where the stars were coming out over the valley that was to be restored. And that for him was enough. He was too old for new and disturbing thoughts.

He turned and followed the young man into the house.

7

This was the fourteenth day. Kumalo said to his wife, "I am going up into the mountain." And she said, "I understand you." For twice before he had done it: once when the small boy Absalom was sick unto death, and once when he had thought of giving up his work as a priest to run a native store at Donnybrook for more money than the church could ever pay.

"Would you come with me," he said, "for I do not like to leave you alone?"

"I cannot come, for the girl is near her time, and who knows when it will be? But you must certainly go."

She made him a bottle of tea and a few heavy cakes of maize. He took his coat and stick and walked up the path that went to the mountain.

Now it was almost dark, and he was alone. But as he started to climb the path that ran through the great stones, a man on a horse was there, and a voice said to him, "It is you, umfundisi?"

"It is I, Mr. Jarvis."

"Well met, umfundisi. For here in my pocket I have a

letter for the people of your church. And the church, umfundisi. Do you desire a new church?" Kumalo could only smile; there were no words in him.

"The plans will shortly come to you, and you must say if they are what you desire. I am anxious to do it quickly, for I shall be leaving this place."

Kumalo stood shocked. And although it was dark, Jarvis understood him, for he said swiftly, "I shall be often here. You know I have work in Ndotsheni. But I am alone in my house, so I am going to Johannesburg to live with my daughter-in-law and her children. You know the small boy?"

"Indeed, I know him."

"Is he like . . . like him?"

"He is like him. There is a brightness inside him."

"Yes, yes, that is true. The other was even so."

They stayed there in silence till Jarvis said, "Umfundisi, where are you going at this hour?"

Kumalo answered, "I am going into the mountain."

"I understand you. I understand completely." Jarvis stretched his hand over the darkening valley, and he said, "One thing is about to be finished, but here is something that is only begun. And while I live it will continue. Umfundisi, go well."

"Sir. Do not go before I have thanked you," said Kumalo. "For the young man, and the milk. And now for the church."

"I give it willingly," said Jarvis. "Go well, umfundisi. Throughout this night, stay well."

And Kumalo cried after him, "Go well, go well."

He climbed to the summit and found a place sheltered from the winds. He began to pray. He prayed for Gertrude and the people of Shanty Town. He gave thanks to God for the kindness of Msimangu and Father Vincent and

Mrs. Lithebe and the white man Jarvis, for the welcome of the people when he returned to Ndotsheni and for the work of restoration now begun.

Why was it given to one man to have so much of his pain changed into gladness?

He woke with a start. It was cold. He thought of his son Absalom. Would he be awake, would he be able to sleep, this night before the morning? He cried out, "My son, my son, my son."

.   .   .   .

When he woke again there was a faint change in the east. And now it was time to be awake, for it might be they had wakened his son, and called him to make ready. He found another place where he could look to the east, and if it was true what men said, when the sun came up over the rim, it would be done.

And the east lightened and lightened, till he knew that the time was not far off. And when he expected it, he rose to his feet and took off his hat and laid it down on the earth, and clasped his hands before him. And while he stood there the sun rose in the east.

.   .   .   .   .   .

Yes, it is the dawn that has come. The titihoya wakes from sleep, and goes about its work of forlorn crying. The sun touches the tops of the mountains. The great valley of the Umzimkulu is still in darkness, but the light will come there. Ndotsheni is still in darkness, but the light will come there also. For it is the dawn that has come, as it has come for a thousand centuries, never failing. But when that dawn will come, of our release from the fear of bondage and the bondage of fear, why, that is a secret.

GLOSSARY

T H E words are defined in the senses in which they are used in the book.

The abbreviations used are n. for noun, v. for verb, adj. for adjective, sy. for somebody, sg. for something and esp. for especially.

A

address v.: speak to.

administer v.: do the work of.

Afrikaans: the language of that part of the white people of South Africa descended from the Dutch.

agricultural adj.: having to do with farming.

airport n.: landing ground for aeroplanes.

alert adj.: watchful.

amongst: among.

appreciate v.: understand and feel the importance of a thing.

assistant n: a person who helps.

astray: go astray--wander out of the right way.

awhile: for a short time.

B

barely: only just so much and no more.

beloved: greatly loved.

bewildering: difficult to understand and therefore worrying.

Bible n.: the holy book of the Christians.

bishop: priest of high rank in the Christian church.

bondage: slavery.

boycott: 1. n. an agreement by a group of people to do no business with a person or group of persons. e.g. not to use the buses.

     2. v. to put such an agreement into practice.

C

carpenter: one who makes things from wood.

clasp v.: to hold firmly.

click n.: a short, sharp sound.

clutch v.: to seize or hold tightly.

coarse adj.: rough, not fine.

compound n.: 1. a living-place shut in by a wall.

     2. esp. in South Africa, for the native miners to live in, without their families, under the control of the mine owners.

comprehend v.: understand.

contour n.: 1. a line (on a map) running through places of the same height.

     2. to plough along the contours of a hill—to plough round the hill, not up and down it.

corrupt v.: make sy. or sg. evil.

crippled adj.: unable to walk or work properly because of sg. wrong with the body.

cunning adj.: clever in a deceiving way.

D

dam n.: wall or bank built to keep back and store water.

darkening adj.: becoming dark.

decent adj.: good, not causing shame to others, proper. Decent wages—good, reasonable wages.

decently : properly, well.

demonstrator : one who shows others how sg. is done.

depths : the parts deep down.

deserted : left alone.

desertion n. : going away and leaving sy. or sg. when it is wrong to do so.

desolate adj. : (a place) bare, like a desert, neglected and sad.

desolation n. : state of being neglected, ruined and sad.

diminishing adj. : becoming less.

disaster n. : sudden or great misfortune.

disastrous adj. : causing sudden or great misfortune.

discharge v. : send away free from a law court.

dumb : unable to speak.

dusk : time of half-darkness as daylight is fading.

E

elderly adj. : getting old.

esquire : polite way of addressing a gentleman on a letter.

essay n. : short piece of writing on one subject.

exhausted adj. : completely used up.

exclamation : word(s) or sound cried out suddenly.

expansion : act of becoming larger.

expenditure : the spending of money.

eye to eye : to see eye to eye—to agree.

F

fare n. : the charge for a journey by bus, train, etc.

fashion v. : to shape, to make.

fiction : sg. which is imagined, a story.

forlorn : cheerless, sad, without hope.

frail : weak, easily broken.

frankly : freely, honestly.

fro: see *to and fro*
frown v.: look angry or puzzled.

G

gamble v.: play games (cards) for money.
gang n.: 1. group of men working together.
    2. esp. group of law-breakers.
gloomy: sad, in low spirits.
goal: a place or idea or thing aimed at.
go well: Zulu way of saying goodbye to one who is going.
gravely: seriously.
grim: having a hard, unpleasant appearance.
growl: 1. v. make low sound in throat like that of angry animal.
    2. n. the sound thus made.

H

halt v.: stop.
harshly: roughly, cruelly, without feeling.
headlines: the title, printed in big letters, of a newspaper article.
headquarters: the chief offices of an organization.
hearty: high-spirited.
hostile: acting like an enemy.
housebreaker: a thief who breaks into houses.
hymn n.: a holy song, usually sung in church.

I

ignorant: having no knowledge.
incorruptible adj.: unable to be made to do evil.
incorruptibility n.: being incorruptible.

indignation : anger caused by another person's wrong doing.

inheritor : one who receives sg. from people from whom he is descended.

innocence n. : knowing nothing of evil.

intervene : come in between.

investigate : enquire into, examine.

J

jerk : make a sudden movement.

jest v. : joke.

jolly : happy, merry.

K

knock sy. *out* : knock sy. unconscious.

knowing adj. : clever, confident, in a tricky way.

L

labour n : 1. work.
     2. workers.

licence n. : official permission (on paper) to do sg.

liquor : strong drink.

loose adj. : to live a loose life—to live a bad life.

lorry : open motor car for carrying goods.

M

madden v. : make very angry, make mad.

magistrate : official acting as judge in lowest courts.

maize : Indian corn.

manuscript : a book written by hand.

marvel v. : think wonderful.

mischief : wrongdoing.

mission : a group of persons (and here, the house they live in)
   working to spread their religion in a district.

mist : cloud of water in drops smaller than raindrops, near the
   ground.

muddled : not clear, not well arranged.

multitude : a very large number.

mute adj. : silent, unable to speak.

N

non- : Latin for "not" and joined to another word, e.g. non-
   European.

O

obstacle : sg. in one's way which prevents movement.

outnumber v. : be more in number than.

overwhelm : cover or swallow up completely.

P

panelling : wooden covering of a wall.

pasture n. : grassland for cattle.

pavement : raised path for walking at side of street in a town.

people n. : esp. family, relatives.

permissible : allowed.

perplexity : difficulty in understanding.

physically : having to do with the body.

pitiless adj.: without pity.

plank n.: a board; a long flat piece of wood.

ponder: think carefully and deeply.

post office book: book recording savings in Post Office Bank.

press v.: to press a person—to urge him.

prostitute n.: woman who sleeps with men for money.

R

range n.: the distance a gun shoots.

rank n.: bus rank· ·a line of buses.

rattle v.: move and make noise like stones shaken in a tin.

reassure: make a person confident again.

rebellion: a rising against the Government.

recover: get better, e.g. after being unwell.

recreation: rest or amusement after work.

recruited: employed for training in some work.

reform v.: change and make better.

reformatory n.: special school where young wrongdoers are trained to be good citizens.

regain: get possession of again.

repayment: sg. given in return for sg.

reproach v.: blame.

resources: wealth and goods of a person or country.

restoration n.: a building up again.

restore v.: put sg. back as it was.

Reverend (Rev): the title of a priest, meaning "respected".

revolver: small gun holding several shots.

rim: edge of a circular thing.

rosy adj.: of light red colour.

rosy-cheeked adj.: having a light red face.

rubbish: waste matter, sg. thrown away as useless.

rumoured: said in common talk, perhaps true, perhaps not.

S

scandal : a shameful thing or action.

sentence v. : to declare in court the punishment for a guilty prisoner.

shabbiness : state of being worn, dirty, in bad repair.

shanty : a poor, roughly built hut for living in.

shilling : in the old British currency 20 shillings = 1 pound.

shiver v. : to shake, as with cold or fear.

shyly : without much confidence in oneself.

solemn : serious and formal.

spark n. : small piece of burning matter.

stammer v. : speak with many hesitations.

stay well : Zulu way, for person who is going, to say goodbye.

strike n. and v. : stopping of work by workers to get better conditions from employers.

string them up : kill them by hanging (slang).

study n. : room in which sy. reads, writes and studies.

stumble : make a wrong step and fall.

suburb : outlying district of a town.

sullen : silently ill-tempered.

summit : the top.

superstition : belief in magic.

survey v. : measure land and make a plan of it.

T

talent : a natural power of the mind, ability.

thoughtless : careless, not considering others.

timidly : in a frightened way.

to and fro : backwards and forwards.

tops : (here) the tops of the hills.

torment : 1. n. severe pain.
　　　　2. v. cause severe pain to.

tormented : made to suffer severe pain.

torture v. : cause great pain to.

touch v. : to have an effect on sy's feelings.

tour n. : a journey in which a number of places are visited.

trade union : organization of workers to get better conditions.

tragedy : sad event, serious accident or crime.

tragic adj. : having the quality of tragedy.

trousers : man's garments covering the legs.

truck : open motor car for carrying goods.

tunnel n. : an underground passage.

U

umfundisi : Zulu for priest, a title of respect.

uncountable adj. : too many to be counted.

undertaking n. : a promise.

uniform n. : special dress which shows what work sy. does. (e.g. soldier, policeman, nurse.)

unmistakable : impossible to mistake.

V

vaguely : uncertainly.

veld : the open grass country of South Africa.

W

wail v. : cry out with grief.

wearily : in a tired manner.

welfare : health, good condition.

withdraw : go away in order to leave sy. or sg.

Y

youngster : a child.

Z

Zulu : a famous tribe of South Africa.